'Do you want me to kiss you?'

Hannah let out a little laugh. 'You're a man of some experience, I should think. Can't you tell?'

He laughed back, softly. 'Yes, I can tell.'

She was innocent—even naive, yes—but she knew what was going on. Knew what Sergei wanted…and what she wanted. Hannah wanted him too much to care if she seemed transparent, obvious, *eager*. She wanted this, but she still would prefer him to take the lead.

And Sergei did just that, sliding his hands under her hair, drawing her closer. She came willingly, even as her heart thudded hard and her head fell back and she waited for the feel of his mouth on hers…

Kate Hewitt discovered her first Mills & Boon® romance on a trip to England when she was thirteen, and she's continued to read them ever since.

She wrote her first story at the age of five, simply because her older brother had written one and she thought she could do it too. That story was one sentence long—fortunately, they've become a bit more detailed as she's grown older.

She has written plays, short stories, and magazine serials for many years, but writing romance remains her first love. Besides writing, she enjoys reading, travelling, and learning to knit.

After marrying the man of her dreams—her older brother's childhood friend—she lived in England for six years and now resides in Connecticut, with her husband, her three young children, and the possibility of one day getting a dog.

Kate loves to hear from readers—you can contact her through her website: www.kate-hewitt.com

Recent titles by the same author:

MR AND MISCHIEF
BOUND TO THE GREEK

KHOLODOV'S LAST MISTRESS

BY
KATE HEWITT

All the characters in this book have no existence outside the imagination of the author, and have no relation whatsoever to anyone bearing the same name or names. They are not even distantly inspired by any individual known or unknown to the author, and all the incidents are pure invention.

First published in Great Britain 2011
by Mills & Boon, an imprint of Harlequin (UK) Limited,
Eton House, 18-24 Paradise Road, Richmond, Surrey TW9 1SR

© Kate Hewitt 2011

ISBN: 978 0 263 88705 1

Harlequin (UK) policy is to use papers that are natural, renewable and recyclable products and made from wood grown in sustainable forests. The logging and manufacturing process conform to the legal environmental regulations of the country of origin.

Printed and bound in Spain
by Blackprint CPI, Barcelona

KHOLODOV'S
LAST MISTRESS

CHAPTER ONE

SHE was about to be pickpocketed. Sergei Kholodov watched with an experienced and jaundiced eye as three street urchins thrust a bunch of newspapers into the face of the foreign girl. Or woman rather; he judged her to be in her early twenties. With her straight teeth and hair and bright red parka, she was definitely American.

She'd been standing in front of St Basil's Cathedral, gazing up at the swirled onion domes with a map forgotten in her hand when they approached her, speaking urgently, pushing the papers. He knew how it went. She obviously didn't. She laughed a little, took a step back, her hands batting the papers, and smiled. *Smiled.* She had no sense whatsoever.

The kids must have seen that. If it was apparent to him, standing twenty metres away, it had to be utterly obvious to them. She'd been chosen for that reason; she was an easy target. They kept the papers close to her face, surrounding her. He heard her laugh again and say in clumsy Russian, '*Spasiba, spasiba, nyet...*'

Sergei's eyes narrowed as one of the urchins darted around and slipped his hand into the pocket of the girl's parka. He knew how quick and quiet you could be when you slid your hand into someone's pocket, grasping fingers reaching for the solid leather bulk of a wallet, the comforting crispness of folded bills. He knew the thrill of danger and the satisfaction—mixed with scorn—of a successful lift.

Suppressing a sigh, Sergei decided he'd better intervene. He had no great love of Americans, but the woman was young and clearly had no idea she was about to be parted from her cash. He strode quickly towards her, the tourists and hucksters parting instinctively for him.

He grabbed the kid who'd had his hand in her pocket by the scruff of his worn and dirty sweatshirt, watched with grim satisfaction as his feet pedalled uselessly through the air. The other kids ran. Sergei felt a stab of pity for the one he'd caught; his friends had been quick to abandon him. He gave him a little shake.

'*Pokazhite mne.*' Give it to me.

'*Spasiba, spasiba,*' the boy protested. 'I don't have anything.'

Sergei felt a hand, gentle yet surprisingly strong, on his shoulder. 'Please,' the woman said in badly accented Russian, 'leave him alone.'

'He was stealing from you,' Sergei replied without turning. He shook the boy again. '*Pokazhite mne!*' The girl's grip strengthened, shoving his shoulder. It didn't hurt, but he was surprised enough that his hold on the boy loosened for a mere second. The street urchin made good use of what he surely knew was his only chance at freedom. He kicked out and connected with Sergei's groin—causing him to swear—and then ran for it.

Sergei drew in a deep breath, forcing himself to block the pain that was ricocheting through his mid-region. He straightened and turned to the woman who had the gall to stare at him with a particularly annoying brand of self-righteous indignation. 'Satisfied?' he queried sardonically, in English, and her eyes—a startling shade of violet—widened in surprise.

'You speak English.'

'Better than you speak Russian,' Sergei informed her. 'Why did you intervene? You'll never get your money back now.'

She frowned. 'My money?'

'That kid you were so kindly defending was pickpocketing you.'

Her expression cleared and she smiled and shook her head. 'No, no, you're mistaken. He was just trying to sell me a newspaper. I would have bought one too, but I can't read Russian *that* well. They were a little overeager,' she allowed, clearly trying to sound fair, and Sergei could not keep the incredulity from showing in his face. Could someone really be so naive? She frowned again, noticing his expression. 'You know that word?'

'Yes, I know that word, and a few others besides. They weren't overeager, lady, they were conning you.' He arched his eyebrows. 'You know *that* word?'

She looked startled, and a little offended, but she let it go, shaking her head wryly. 'Sorry. I know my Russian's awful. But I really don't think those kids were up to any harm.'

Sergei's mouth thinned. 'Check, then.'

'Check…?'

'Check your pockets.'

She shook her head again, still smiling, still naive. 'Honestly, they were just trying to—'

'Check.'

Her eyes flashed indigo and for a moment Sergei saw something under the sweetness, something powerful and raw, and he felt a flicker of interest. Maybe even of lust. She was quite pretty, with those violet eyes and heart-shaped face. With that bulky parka he couldn't see much else. Then she shrugged, smiling in good-natured defeat, and spread her hands. 'Fine, if you want me to prove it to…' Her voice trailed off as she reached into her pockets, and Sergei watched the emotions flash across her face. Confusion, impatience, uncertainty, disbelief, outrage. He'd seen the progression a thousand times before, usually from afar with a half dozen twenties in his fist.

Except, he realised as he watched her closely, she wasn't outraged. Hurt, maybe, by the way her eyes darkened to the colour of storm clouds, but then she shook her head again in that accepting way of hers that both annoyed and affected him and shrugged. 'You're right. They took my cash.'

Why was she so good-natured? 'Why,' Sergei asked in as reasonable a tone as he could manage, 'did you keep cash in your pocket?'

She pulled her lower lip between her teeth, and his narrowed gaze was drawn to that innocent action. Again he felt that flicker. Her lips were full and rosebud-pink, and something about the way she nipped at them with those straight white American teeth made his middle clench. Or maybe lower down. Irritation and interest, annoyance and attraction.

'I'd just been to the bank,' she said, her tone one of explanation rather than defence. 'I hadn't had time to put it away—'

She'd been standing staring at St Basil's with a map dangling forgotten from her hand. She'd had plenty of time. But why should he care? Sergei asked himself. Why should he bother even having this conversation? She was just another American tourist. He'd seen plenty of those over the years, from the first ones who goggled at the pathetic obscurity of an actual Russian orphan to the ones who judged with an assessing eye and brought in an army of therapists and psychologists to make sure no child was too *damaged*. As if they had any idea. And then of course tourists like this woman, who swarmed Red Square and gazed at the Kremlin and the GUM department store and all the rest as if everything were no more than a bizarre and rather quaint antiquity, rather than a lasting witness to his country's heart-wrenching history. He had no time for any of them, and certainly not for her. He'd already half turned away when he heard her soft little exhalation of dismay, no more than a breath, as if she wouldn't allow herself any more.

Sergei turned back. 'What?'

'My passport…'

'You kept your passport in your coat *pocket*?'

'I told you, I'd just been to the bank…'

'Your passport,' Sergei repeated, because he honestly couldn't believe someone would actually keep their cash and passport in an unzipped coat pocket while they walked across Red Square.

She smiled ruefully now, acknowledging his incredulity, accepting it even. 'I know, I know. But I was cashing my traveller's cheques and they needed ID—'

'Traveller's cheques,' Sergei repeated. This got better and better. Or worse and worse, depending how you looked at it. He'd thought with the advent of computer banking those cheques had become obsolete. 'Why on earth were you using traveller's cheques? Why not an ATM card?' Much simpler. Less chance of being stolen. Unless, of course, you kept the card in your coat pocket, with the pin number kindly attached with Sellotape to the back, as this woman probably would. Just to help a thief out.

She lifted her chin, and he saw that flare of indigo again. 'I prefer traveller's cheques.'

Now he was the one to shrug. 'Fine.' And he would have turned away, he would have turned away so quickly and easily, if not for the way her smile faltered, her lips trembling, and he saw desolation cloud her eyes to a grey-violet, the long lashes sweeping downwards to hide the sorrow he'd already seen there. He felt a painful twist in the region of his heart, a kind of raw emotion he didn't like feeling, hadn't let himself feel in years. Yet somehow with one sorrowful look she hadn't even wanted him to see, he felt it. And it made him furious.

* * *

Hannah knew it had been rather foolish of her to carry her cash and passport in the front pocket of her coat; she *got* that. She would have put it away in her zipped purse except she'd become distracted by the beauty of St Basil's, its colourful domes piercing the hard blue of the sky. And, she acknowledged, she'd been thinking about how today was her last day of travel, how tomorrow she'd be back in upstate New York, opening the shop, taking inventory, trying to make things *work*. And while she'd known it shouldn't have, the thought gave her a little pang of—sorrow? Regret? Something like that. Something she pushed away, didn't want to feel.

And now this Russian…*assassin* was looking at her with daggers in his ice-blue eyes. Hannah didn't know what he did for a living, but the man was seriously intimidating. He wore a black leather coat over black jeans, not exactly the friendliest of outfits. His hair was a relatively ordinary brown but it was cut very short and framed a face so coldly arresting that Hannah's heart had near stopped in her chest when he'd approached her.

And now *this*…the last of her money gone. Her passport gone. And her flight back to New York left in five hours.

'What?' the man asked brusquely. He'd turned back to her, impatience and irritation evident in every taut line of his well-muscled body. The man radiated lethal, barely leashed power. Yet still he'd turned back, even it seemed as if he'd done so against his will, or at least his better judgment. 'You know you'll need to go to your embassy, don't you?'

'Yes…'

'They'll help you,' he explained to her, slowly, as if she had trouble understanding her own language. 'They can issue you a new passport.'

'Right.' She swallowed. 'How long does that usually take, do you know?'

'A few hours to fill out the paperwork, I should think.' He arched an eyebrow. 'Does that inconvenience you?'

'It does, actually,' she informed him, managing a wry smile despite the panic plunging icily in her stomach. She was starting to realise how awful this really was. No passport. No money. Missing her flight. In Moscow.

All bad.

'Perhaps you should have thought of that when you wandered around Red Square,' the man returned. 'You might as well have hung a placard around your neck declaring you were a tourist, ripe for the taking.'

'I *am* a tourist,' Hannah pointed out in what she thought was quite a reasonable tone. 'And I don't know why it's got you so worked up. It's not your money, or your passport.'

The man stared at her, his expression turning from fierce to something close to bewildered. 'You're right,' he said after a moment. 'There's no reason for me to be worked up at all.' Yet he didn't turn away as she'd half expected him to, just kept staring at her as if she were a puzzle he couldn't quite solve.

'In any case,' Hannah said, 'I don't mind that they took my money.' Well, she wouldn't have minded, except that it was the only money she'd had left. And as for the passport... She lifted her chin, staring the man down. Sort of. 'They need it more than I do, and at least now they can buy food—'

'You think they're going to buy food?'

She shook her head. 'Don't tell me they must be buying drugs or something awful like that. Even children who live on the street need to eat, and they couldn't have been more than twelve—'

'Twelve is plenty old on the street,' the man informed her. 'And food is easy enough to score, just steal from a fruit and vegetable stall or wait out in the back of a restaurant. You don't use *money* to buy food. Not unless you have to.'

Hannah stared at him, surprised by his knowing tone, discomfited by the fierce light in those ice-blue eyes. 'Sorry,' she muttered. 'And thanks for helping me out. If you hadn't come along—well, if I hadn't interfered, maybe I'd still have my money.' And her passport.

The man jerked his head in a semblance of a nod. 'You'll go to your embassy?' he asked, sounding almost as if the words—the concern—were forced from him. 'You know where it is?'

'Yes.' She didn't, but she wasn't going to give this man any more reasons to think her an idiot. 'Thank you for helping me out.'

'Good luck,' he said after a moment, and, nodding her own farewell, Hannah turned and started walking across Red Square.

Now that she was no longer dealing with that man and his forceful presence, the panic lodged icily in the pit of her stomach was becoming heavier. Icier. She swallowed, squared her shoulders—just in case he was watching—and strode towards the other side of the square. She'd look at her map then, and figure out where the American Embassy was.

Two hours later she'd finally reached the window in the consular department of the American Embassy, only to be rather flatly told that she had to report the theft to the Moscow Police Department, fill out a form, and bring it back to the embassy before she reapplied for a passport.

'Reapply,' Hannah repeated, not liking the word. She'd been hoping—praying—that they could just give her some sort of stamped form, like a get-out-of-jail-free card that would let her on the aeroplane. Get her home.

The woman behind the window looked at her without a flicker of sympathy or interest. To be fair, Hannah told herself, she probably heard this kind of sob story all the time. And it wasn't her job to help Hannah, just give the information. Still, Hannah had to swallow past the lump in her throat as she explained, 'But my flight leaves tonight.'

'Reschedule,' the woman said. 'It will take days to get a passport, and after that you have to reapply for your entry visa.'

An entry visa? 'But I'm *leaving.*'

She shrugged. 'Your Russian contact will have to vouch for you.' She passed a paper under the window and Hannah stared at it, saw the hundred-dollar fee for a passport application.

'My contact is just a hotel,' Hannah said, desperation now edging her voice. 'I don't think—'

'Talk to the police,' the woman advised. 'You must do that first.' Already she was looking over Hannah's shoulder, indicating that the next person should come forward.

'But—' Hannah leaned forward, flushing as she spoke in a whisper '—I don't have any money.'

Still no sympathy. 'Use the ATM. Or a credit card.'

Of course. That was the normal, expected thing to do. Except she didn't have that much money in the bank to withdraw, and she'd cut up her credit cards after seeing the bills her parents had racked up before their deaths. Maybe not the wisest decision, but now that she'd finally paid the bills off she'd been determined never to be in debt again. The woman must have seen something of this in her face for she said, a touch impatiently, 'Call someone, then. In America. They can wire you money.'

'Right.' It was finally sinking in just what kind of trouble she was in. 'Thank you for your time,' she said, and fortunately her voice didn't wobble.

'Any time,' the woman said in a bored voice, and the next person started forward.

Hannah walked slowly outside; there was a chill to the spring air now, and the sky had darkened to a steely grey.

She was really trying hard not to panic. She normally wasn't a panicker, tried to see the best in everything and everyone.

Only now it was getting dark and she had no money, no passport, no options. She could call a friend, as the woman had advised, but Hannah resisted that option. She'd have to reverse the charges of the telephone call, and then explain her awful predicament, and then whomever she called—and no names sprang readily to mind—would have to drive fifty miles to Albany to wire the money, and that money would have to be hundreds of dollars at the very least. Passport fees, hotel stays, food, perhaps even another plane ticket. It could be *thousands* of dollars.

She didn't have friends with that kind of money, and she didn't have that kind of money either. She'd used the last of her own savings to fund this trip, knowing it was foolish, impulsive, everything she never was. Except maybe she *was* foolish, and stupid even, as that man in Red Square had so obviously thought, because if she had any sense at all she wouldn't be standing on the steps of the American Embassy, people and traffic streaming indifferently, impatiently all around her, with no place to go, no idea what she could do. Nothing.

She swallowed the panic that had started in her stomach and was now steadily working its way up her throat. She wasn't completely lost. She had a little money in the bank, enough to give her some time—

And then?

'There you are.'

Hannah blinked, focused in the oncoming dusk, and then stared in surprise as the man from Red Square strode towards her, his leather coat billowing blackly out behind him, a scowl on his face. He looked like an avenging angel, his blue eyes blazing determination and maybe a little irritation as well. Still, she could not stem the unreasonable tide of relief and gratitude that washed over her at the sight of him. A familiar face.

'What are you doing here?'

'I wanted to make sure you'd sorted out your papers.'

'That was very kind of you,' she said, cautiously, because three months of travel had taught her to be, if not cynical, then at least sensible. 'And unnecessary.'

'I know.' The corner of his mouth quirked very slightly, so slightly that it couldn't be called a smile in the least. Yet still the sight of it made Hannah feel safer, and stronger, even as she felt a shiver of awareness. He was, she acknowledged, a very attractive man. 'Did you get your passport sorted?' he asked and she shook her head.

'No. I got a form.' She waved the paper half-heartedly. 'Apparently I'm to go to the police department and file a report there.'

'They're all disorganised.' He shook his head in disgust. 'Or corrupt. Usually both. It could take hours.'

'Wonderful.' Her plane left in three hours. Clearly she wasn't going to be on it.

'Do you have any money at all?' the man asked abruptly and Hannah shrugged, not wanting to admit just how much trouble she was in. 'A little,' she said. 'In the bank.' But not enough to pay the passport fee, and a hotel, and meals and other expenses besides. Not nearly enough.

'A credit card?'

He must have been speaking to the woman in the embassy. Or maybe he just knew everything. 'Um...no.'

He shook his head with that rather contemptuous incredulity she was coming to know so well. 'You embark on international travel, to Russia of all places, without even a credit card, and clearly no savings?'

'Put like that, it does sound pretty stupid, doesn't it?' Hannah agreed. She wasn't about to explain how she hadn't wanted this trip to send her into debt, or why she was wary of credit cards. 'It was just,' she explained quietly, 'this trip was kind of a once-in-a-lifetime opportunity.'

He looked sceptical. Of course. 'Really.'

'Yes, really. You have that disdain thing down pat, by the way. I don't think I've been lectured to so much since I was in elementary school.'

He let out a little bark of laughter that surprised her, it was so unexpected. She smiled, glad that he seemed to possess a sense of humour after all. 'I am simply surprised,' he said, his expression turning stern once more. 'Have you been travelling long?'

'Three months.'

'And you have not encountered problems before this?'

'Not as big as this. I was charged double at a restaurant in Italy, and a train conductor was really rude—'

'That is all?'

'I guess I'm lucky. Or at least I was.'

'I suppose,' the man said, 'I shouldn't even ask if you have travel insurance.'

Now *that* hadn't even crossed her mind. Hannah managed a grin. 'Nope.'

He raised his eyebrows. 'Nope, I shouldn't ask, or nope, you don't?'

'Take your pick.'

One tiny corner of his mouth quirked up again, and Hannah felt her heart skip a silly beat. He was intimidating and stern and even a little scary, but he was also incredibly good-looking. Sexy, even, especially when he smiled.

'Were you planning to stay in this country long?'

'Actually, my plane leaves—' she checked her watch '—in two hours.'

He stared at her, eyebrows arched in incredulity. 'Today is your last day?'

'Apparently not. Mother Russia is insisting I stay a little longer. I need an entry visa as well as a passport.'

The man shook his head, clearly rendered speechless by her predicament. Hannah could hardly resent his incredulity. She'd really been rather foolish. And she could have so easily prevented this, as this man had pointed out. A credit card, a zipped pocket, a little more savoir faire.

'You must,' he finally said, 'at least have some friends who could wire you some money.'

'Well, not exactly.' He arched one eyebrow, the gesture saturnine and unbearably eloquent. 'I live in a small town,' Hannah explained. 'And it would be difficult to wire—'

'No one can help you out when you are desperate? I thought small American towns were full of do-gooders. Everyone knows everyone and is willing to help each other out.'

'I think you're thinking of Mayberry,' she said, naming a fictional town in a 1960s television programme where the sun always shone and people ambled down to the drug store for an ice-cream soda.

'So your town isn't like that?'

Hannah didn't like what he was implying. What did he have against her, anyway? Just that she'd been phenomenally stupid and left her passport in her pocket? He seemed bent on a mission to discredit and disillusion her. 'I just have to think about it,' she said evenly. 'And who to call.' Who could and would drive the distance, both literally and figuratively. Ashley, maybe, but with her move and new job she was just getting on her feet financially.

'And while you're thinking…?' He glanced around at the darkening streets, the steady traffic.

'I'll figure something out.' She could fetch her bag from the hotel, find some place cheaper. It was a start, at least. 'Why do you care, anyway?' Hannah eyed him, his close-cut hair, his icy eyes, the overwhelming breadth of his shoulders under all that black leather.

The man's eyes narrowed even as his lips twitched. 'Don't worry,' he told her dryly. 'I have no intention of enacting any of the options that are undoubtedly racing through your terrified mind. Let me introduce myself properly.' He slid a wallet from the inside pocket of his coat—of course he'd keep it *there*—and from it extracted a crisp white business card.

Hannah took the card warily, for, although she wasn't generally a suspicious person, she still had sense. No matter what this man thought. She wasn't going to trust him. Yet, anyway. She glanced down at the card, her eyes widening slightly at the words printed on it in stark black ink. *Sergei Kholodov, CEO, Kholodov Enterprises,* and an address of an office building in Moscow's centre. She handed the card back to him.

'Impressive.' Of course anyone could print up a fake business card, even an expensive-looking one like that. This man could still be a drug dealer or a slave trader or who knew what else. She folded her arms across her chest, conscious of the chilly wind ruffling her hair and cutting through her parka.

'I can see you're not convinced.'

'I'm not sure why you're here.'

'At least you're finally showing some common sense,' he remarked dryly. 'To tell you the truth, I feel a bit responsible for the theft of your things.'

'Why? I was the one who forced you to let that little boy go.'

'You didn't *force* anything,' he told her a bit sharply, and Hannah suppressed a small smile that she'd actually pricked his pride. It made him seem more approachable, if such a thing were possible. She wasn't sure it was.

'Sorry,' she said, her lips twitching. 'I distracted you then from your manly effort.'

He didn't like that either, judging by his scowl. 'I could

have come over sooner,' he told her. 'I saw what those kids were doing.'

'You watched?'

'I waited a moment too long,' he clarified. 'And in any case, you don't have many options.'

That was certainly true. 'I'm still not sure how that affects you,' Hannah said.

'You can stay the night at my hotel. In the morning I can help you sort something out with the police and the embassy.'

He made it sound so simple. Maybe there was a get-out-of-jail-free card after all. 'That's very nice of you,' Hannah said at last. She still felt uncertain, even suspicious. It seemed too easy. Too nice. For him, anyway. 'What hotel?' she finally asked as her mind considered and discarded non-existent possibilities.

'The Kholodov.'

'*The* Kholodov?' It was one of the most luxurious hotels in Moscow, and way, way out of her budget. And he, she recalled from the card, was Sergei Kholodov. *That* Kholodov.

Now his mouth kicked up at one corner, and even though it still wasn't really a smile it transformed his face, lightening his eyes, softening his features, so Hannah felt a sudden blazing bolt of awareness ignite her senses. When he smiled he really did look *amazing*.

'You've heard of it.'

'Hasn't everyone?'

He shrugged even as his mouth quirked a little more, revealing a surprising dimple. The assassin had a dimple. She felt another bolt of awareness, as if her senses had been struck by lightning. It wasn't, she decided, an unpleasant sensation. Not at all.

'So,' he said, 'you might as well stay there.'

Hannah hesitated. She believed in the best of people, wanted to believe in the best in him. She just didn't want to be even more foolish than she'd already been. 'It's very nice of you to offer—'

'If you're worried about security, you can take a taxi yourself to the hotel. I'll pay for the fare.'

'You don't—'

He arched an eyebrow. '*You* don't have any money, do you? And trust me, it is no trouble. I have empty rooms. I have plenty of money. And,' he added, glancing at his watch, 'I have things to do. So make up your mind.'

When he put it like that, it sounded sensible. And surely her best option. 'Okay,' Hannah said at last. 'Thank you.'

'I told you, it is no trouble.' Sergei stretched one arm out towards the street and within seconds a taxi cab had screeched to a halt in front of him. Sergei dismissed it, and the next one he flagged as well, explaining tersely, 'They're both unmarked. You'll feel safer in an official taxi, with a meter.' His consideration for such a detail touched her.

Finally a legit taxi pulled to the kerb, and Sergei opened the door. 'The Kholodov,' he told the driver, handing him a wad of rubles. He glanced at Hannah. 'I'll phone and make sure they're expecting you. We can get your bags sent over later. Is that sufficient?'

Sufficient? It was crazy. Yet she understood what he was asking, that he was taking these measures to make her feel safe, and she appreciated it more than she could put into words. He'd saved her, quite literally. 'Thank you. I don't know what to—'

'Go.' He practically pushed her towards the cab, and then slammed the door as soon as she'd slid into the seat.

'Say,' she finished in a whisper as the cab sped away into the darkness and she wondered if she'd ever see her saviour again.

CHAPTER TWO

'You wanted to know about the girl?'

Sergei glanced up from the papers he'd been scanning to scowl at his assistant, Grigori. The girl... Hannah Pearl, he'd discovered with a little bit of research, lone traveller, ditzy American. He did *not* want to know about the girl—even if he hadn't been able to get her out of his mind since he'd sent her off in a taxi two hours ago. He'd come back to his office, changed out of the street clothes he wore whenever he went to the unsavoury areas of the city in search of Varya. He hadn't found her; he'd found a beguiling American instead.

Even now he found himself thinking about the violet of her eyes, those rose-pink lips. He wondered what kind of figure her bulky parka had hid. But even more so than her physical charms, of which he acknowledged she had several, he'd been bizarrely fascinated—and irritated—by her honesty. Her optimism. She'd seemed so...unspoiled. When had he last encountered a person—a woman—like that?

'She's settled?' he asked tersely. That was all he needed to know.

'Yes, in the grand suite.'

He'd given her the best room in the hotel. Stupid, perhaps, and unnecessary, but he hadn't liked seeing her looking so lost as she stood on the steps of the embassy. He hated seeing people vulnerable, hated seeing that shadow of uncertainty and fear in someone's eyes. He'd seen it far too often. And for a moment, a crazy, regrettable moment, the American had actually reminded him of Alyona. And he *never* thought of Alyona.

Yet in that moment on the steps when Hannah's eyes had clouded and she'd lifted her chin—seeming, for an instant, so *brave*—she *had* reminded him, and it had made him approach her, offer things he'd had no intention of offering. Feel things he didn't want to feel.

Of course, he'd already made the decision to find her at the embassy when he'd seen her on the steps, felt that protective tug. When she'd walked away from him in Red Square he'd felt something else he didn't like to feel: guilt. He'd watched those kids run their grift and he could have stopped it sooner. Maybe if he had, if he hadn't taken those few scornful seconds to just *watch,* she'd still have her money and passport. She'd be on a plane back to America, instead of upstairs in the best room of his hotel.

Upstairs...

Now his mind—and body—went in a totally different direction. He didn't feel protective so much as...possessive. He was curious about the body hidden beneath that parka, those eyes that darkened to storm when she felt something other than that relentless optimism. Curious and also determined that the only thing this woman would awaken in him was lust.

Impulsively, yet with iron-like decisiveness, he reached for a piece of heavy ivory stationery embossed with the Kholodov crest and scrawled a message. Folding it, he handed it to Grigori with a level look that ensured no more questions would be asked. 'Deliver that to her. And prepare the private booth at the restaurant for dinner. For two.'

Grigori nodded and hesitated by the door. 'You found Varya?' he asked and Sergei let out a heavy sigh.

'No.' He'd been too distracted by a certain American to

devote any more time to his search for Varya. He knew she
was in trouble again; the tearful, incoherent message on his
private voice mail had given testament to that. Yet when was
Varya not in trouble?

'She'll turn up again,' Grigori said, and Sergei knew he
was trying to convince himself more than Sergei. The three of
them had banded together back in the orphanage, and Grigori,
Sergei suspected, was more than half in love with Varya, and
had been since they were children. 'She always does.'

'Yes.' Yet he did not want Varya to turn up as a nameless,
disease-riddled corpse forgotten in a doorway or floating in
the Moskva River. But how many times could he save her?
He'd already learned to his own frustration and sometimes
despair how few people you could really save. Sometimes not
even yourself.

Grigori held up the note, and Sergei half regretted his im-
pulse to write it. 'I'll deliver this now.' He nodded his assent,
knowing it was too late for regrets. And better that he put
Hannah Pearl in her place as a woman to be desired and discarded rather than anything else. Anything deeper.

A woman who made him think of Alyona, and remember
the kind of boy he'd once been, as youthful and naive as she
so obviously still was.

No, Sergei thought as he gazed moodily out at a darkening sky, this was much better.

Hannah gazed around the gorgeous hotel suite, half afraid
to touch anything. The place was amazing. And huge. She'd
actually thought the closet was another bedroom, until she'd
realised there was no bed in it.

What kind of man was Sergei Kholodov anyway?

A tremor ran through her, something half between alarm
and excitement. He was *that* kind of man. She might not have
a lot of experience when it came to men—Hadley Springs

didn't have a great dating scene—but she still recognised her own reaction. There was something so blatantly sexy about Sergei Kholodov, the way he emanated all that authority, the iciness of his eyes, the leashed power of his body. She'd never been with a more exciting person. *Man.*

Yet it hardly mattered, because Hannah doubted she'd ever see him again. His kindness was already more than Hannah had ever expected. So why was she still thinking about him?

It was hard *not* to think of him. The events of the last few hours had been both surreal and overwhelming, from the first moment that Sergei had strode across Red Square, to seeing him outside the American Embassy, to entering his amazing and opulent hotel. It was the stuff of fantasies, of soap operas, not the life of a very ordinary woman from a tiny town in upstate New York. Nothing like this had happened to her for the entire three months of her trip, and now on the last day her world was spinning.

Well, hopefully it would settle right back on its axis tomorrow, when Sergei helped her get a passport and a plane out of here.

Did that mean she *would* see him again?

Hannah decided not to overthink it. She was going to take this crazy ride, enjoy it as much as possible, and it would all end tomorrow when life—God willing—returned to normal. Right now she wanted a good, long soak in the swimming-pool-size sunken tub she'd seen in the bathroom.

Her suitcase, amazingly, had arrived in her room shortly after she'd got there. Hannah had no idea how Sergei had arranged that; she hadn't even told him her name, much less the hotel at which she'd been staying. The man definitely had some serious power. Still, she was glad to have her things and she was just unzipping the single case when a discreet knock sounded at the door.

Hannah tensed, felt that flip of excitement and alarm.

Running a quick hand over her hair, she hurried to the door and peered through the peephole, suppressing a ridiculous stab of disappointment that it wasn't Sergei.

She opened the door to a slight, serious-looking man in a sober suit. A port-wine birthmark covered half his face, and he blinked with a kind of short-sighted owlishness.

'Miss Pearl, my name is Grigori and I am Mr Kholodov's personal assistant. I have a missive for you from him.'

A *missive*? It sounded important. Hannah took the folded paper the man had handed to her. 'Thank you.'

'May I give him your reply?'

'Oh…right.' Quickly, fumbling a bit, she unfolded the paper and scanned the two lines that had been written in a bold black scrawl. *Please join me for dinner in the hotel restaurant at eight. Sergei.*

She swallowed, looked up, saw Grigori waiting. Well, she *did* need to eat. And a public restaurant was a safe and fairly innocuous place. And she was curious, and excited, and a little nervous. It seemed this crazy ride had a few more dips and turns. Why on earth did Sergei Kholodov want to have dinner with her? Was he just being nice or…?

'Miss Pearl?'

'Okay. Yes. Thank you. I'd be—ah—happy to join Mr Kholodov at eight.'

'Very good.' Grigori snapped his heels together military-style and turned to leave.

'Grigori—'

He turned back. 'Yes, Miss Pearl?'

'Is— That is—' She swallowed, her mouth suddenly dry. 'Has Mr Kholodov owned this hotel for very long?' She wanted to know *something* about this enigmatic man, something his assistant would be willing to answer.

Grigori frowned slightly. 'I believe it has been five years,

Miss Pearl. There is a pamphlet in the desk drawer concerning the history of the hotel, if you are interested.'

'Okay. Great. Thanks.' Smiling awkwardly, Hannah closed the door. Still dazed by the sudden and entirely unexpected invitation, she went to the desk and took out the pamphlet. She skimmed the paragraphs about the historic building, how it had been a hotel for a hundred years, had fallen into disrepair and been abandoned. Her interest sharpened when she read that Sergei had bought and renovated it, provided jobs for a thousand people, and was committed to the highest service possible.

He really was an incredible man. And she was going to have dinner with him. Her heart began to thump, her tummy turning somersaults. She was going to have dinner with Sergei Kholodov. It wasn't a date, of course. She understood that. A man like Sergei Kholodov couldn't actually be interested in her…could he?

Was she ridiculous to wonder even for a moment that he might? An icy thrill ran like cold fire through her veins at the thought. Then she realised with a flutter of something between dismay and desolation that she had nothing to wear.

Hannah straightened. She could hardly hope to impress someone of Sergei Kholodov's wealth and experience. And it was only dinner after all.

By seven-thirty Hannah was dressed and ready. She gazed at herself in the mirror, acknowledging that the simple black dress in soft jersey was flattering but also plain, and three months in a rucksack hadn't done it any favours. Fortunately the material had mostly smoothed out, and she liked the simple style, ending in a swirl around her calves. Her only jewellery was a single string of pearls her parents had given her for her eighteenth birthday. She finished the outfit with low black pumps, a slick of lip gloss, and then she was done.

Now she just had to wait half an hour. She definitely didn't want to appear overeager, especially since he *knew* that word. Her lips twitched at the memory. She must have seemed terribly patronising, especially considering how excellent his English was.

She flicked through a few of the television channels, trying to settle her still flip-flopping stomach, until five minutes to eight when she made her way back down to the sumptuous lobby. Not overeager, just punctual.

The restaurant was understated, elegant, and buzzing with people. Hannah stood uncertainly in the doorway, looking around for Sergei, for no more than a few seconds before she felt a sure touch at her elbow.

'Miss Pearl? Mr Kholodov is waiting for you.'

Hannah turned to see Grigori. He smiled at her, shyly, and Hannah thought how different he was from Sergei. She wondered if his boss scared him with his scowls and sneers, or if he was used to it. Or did Sergei Kholodov just scowl at her?

'Miss Pearl?' he prompted, and Hannah realised she'd just been standing there, staring into space. And Sergei was waiting. Somehow she didn't think he liked to wait. She swallowed, nodding, and followed Grigori through the dining room to a discreet alcove in the back, part of the main dining room and yet also quite private. No one could see into this secluded and intimate corner. A table with an L-shaped banquette in plush crimson velvet was laid with crystal, flickering with candlelight. Sergei slid out of the booth as she approached, and now stood in front of her, his gaze sweeping over her in a brief but thorough assessment.

Her face—her whole body—heated under his gaze. She didn't think she was imagining a look like that. And yet the thought that he might actually find her attractive was incredible, impossible. Exciting.

He looked, she thought as the thud of her heart seemed to roar in her ears, amazing. He'd exchanged the leather trench

coat and jeans for a well-cut silk suit in a charcoal grey, and
it did even better things for his shoulders, if that were possible. She couldn't keep herself from noticing the strong lines
of his body: his jaw, his shoulder, his thigh. The man was a
painting, or perhaps a sculpture.

'Good evening,' he said, and Hannah very nearly bobbed
a curtsey back. She felt so out of her element, and no more so
than when Sergei slowly reached out a hand, which she took
instinctively, and with a sensual smile led her to the table.

Sergei saw Hannah's eyes widen and flare and felt a shaft of
desire stab him as she bit her lip, taking its rosy fullness between her teeth, her wide-eyed gaze taking in the obvious intimacy of their surroundings. Just looking at her he felt desire
flood through his veins, fire his resolve. He wanted her, and
that made things simple. Lust was easy, desire safe. And as
her gaze finally rested on him, open and guileless, he thought
she desired him back. A faint flush tinged her cheeks and she
dropped her hand from where she'd been toying with her hair.

Sergei let his gaze sweep over her once more. Her hair,
last scraped back into a ponytail, now fell almost to her waist
in a rippling chestnut waterfall, the candlelight picking out
strands of amber and gold. Her dress was cheap and boring
but it didn't matter. The fabric draped lovingly over the gentle
curves of her breasts and hips; they were slight and she was
almost too thin, yet Sergei was still tempted. Still speechless.

She wasn't classically beautiful, there was something too
open and honest about her for that; she possessed no haughty
awareness or distance. Yet she still looked breathtaking, and
she was the only woman Sergei had ever met who caused him
to break his rules, to want more, more than he ever let himself want.

He pushed the thought—the want—aside. This was lust,
pure and simple. That was all. He'd make sure of that.

'I hope you found everything in your room comfortable,' he said.

'*Comfortable?* Are you kidding me? It was amazing. The tub alone—I stayed in there for an hour.' She held out her hands for his inspection. 'My fingers are still wrinkled like prunes.'

'I'm glad you enjoyed all the room's amenities,' he said smoothly, and she dropped her hands, laughing a little.

'Definitely. Thank you. This is all so…like something out of a fairy tale. Really.' Her eyes held a playful, teasing light. 'Are you my fairy godmother?'

'No,' Sergei said, 'Just someone assuaging his own guilty conscience.'

'You hardly need to feel guilty,' she said as she slid into the booth. He caught a whiff of her honeyed scent: snowdrops, the signature scent of the complementary toiletries found in every room in his hotel. The scent, he'd always thought, of sweetness and courage.

'Would you like a glass of wine?' he asked, reaching for the bottle of red already open.

'Oh…well. Okay.' She smiled, trying to be sophisticated, clearly nervous. 'Thank you.'

She was, Sergei thought, incredibly open. Those eyes, that face, every word she said…she hid nothing. Having hidden every emotion since he could remember, he was both disturbed and moved by the thought.

He handed her the glass and poured one for himself. 'To unexpected moments,' he said, raising his glass, and after a second's hesitation she self-consciously clinked her glass with his own.

'I've certainly had a few of those today,' she said after she'd taken a tiny sip of wine.

'So tell me about this trip of yours,' Sergei said as he sat next to her. 'This once-in-a-lifetime opportunity.'

'Well…' She paused, frowning faintly. 'My parents died. They were elderly, and it wasn't unexpected, but it was all kind of…intense, and I decided afterwards that this was an opportunity to take some time out for myself.' She gave him a wry smile. 'Even if I didn't have any savings.'

'I'm sorry about your parents,' he said quietly. Her admission had given him a flicker of surprised sympathy. She was an orphan, of a sort, just as he was. 'Savings aside,' he continued, 'you obviously had enough money to fund the trip at least.'

'Just,' Hannah agreed. 'But it was tight. I had to close the shop, of course, and scrimp quite a bit—' She stopped suddenly, shaking her head ruefully. 'But you don't want to hear about that. Very boring stuff, especially to a millionaire like you.'

Billionaire, actually, but Sergei wasn't about to correct her. He was curious about this shop of hers, and her whole life, and the way she stared at him as if she trusted him, as if she trusted everyone. Hadn't life taught her *anything*? It made him want to destroy her delusions and wrap her in cotton wool all at the same time.

Desirable, he reminded himself. That was it. Simple. Easy.

'You mentioned a shop,' he said. He shifted in his seat and his thigh nudged hers. He saw her eyes widen and she bit the lush fullness of her lip once more.

'Y-yes, a shop,' she said, stammering slightly, and he knew that brief little nudge had affected her. And if that affected her—what would she be like in his arms? In his bed?

Guilt pricked him momentarily, sharp and pointed. Should he really be thinking like this? She had innocence stamped all over her. His lovers were always experienced and even jaded like him, women who understood his rules. Who never tried to get close.

Because if they did…if they ever *knew*…

Sergei pushed the needling sense of guilt away, hardened his heart. And pictured himself slipping that dress from her shoulders, pressing his lips to the pulse fluttering quite wildly at her throat. She wanted him. He wanted her.

Simple.

It was foolish to feel so…aware, Hannah told herself. So *alive*. They were just talking. Yet still she was acutely, achingly conscious of Sergei's thigh just inches from hers, the strength and heat of him right across the table, the candlelight throwing the harsh planes of his face into half-shadow.

'A shop,' she repeated, knowing she must sound as brainless as he'd thought her this morning. 'My parents started it before I was born, and I took it over when they died.'

'What kind of shop?'

'Crafts. Mainly knitting supplies, yarn and so forth, but also embroidery and sewing things. Whatever we—I—think will sell.' Even six months after her mother's death, it was still strange—and sad—to think the shop was hers. Only hers.

'And you had to close the shop? You couldn't have anyone running it while you were away?'

'I can't really afford it,' she said. 'It's a small town and we don't get a lot of business except during tourist season.' And even then just drive-throughs.

'Where is this small town of yours?'

'Hadley Springs, about four hours north of New York City.'

'It must be beautiful.'

'It is.' She loved the rugged beauty of the Adirondacks, the impenetrable pine forests, yet living in a small town as a twenty-something could get a bit lonely, something she thought Sergei surmised from the shrewd compassion in his narrowed eyes.

'You have not wanted to move?'

'No, nev—' Hannah stopped suddenly, for she couldn't

actually say she hadn't *wanted* it; it had simply never been an option. Her parents had needed her too much, the shop needed to be run, and she couldn't imagine abandoning it all now. The shop had been everything to them, and she needed to make a go of it, for the sake of their memory at least. She knew it was what her parents would have wanted, even expected. And yet… 'I don't even know where I would go,' she said after a moment, trying to shrug the question—and the sudden doubts it had made her have—away.

Sergei's smile glinted in the candlelight. 'Possibility can be a frightening thing.'

'I suppose,' she said slowly, thinking that it never had been before. She hadn't let herself think about possibilities, yet somehow sitting in this candlelit room with this breathtakingly attractive man gazing at her so steadily made everything—and anything—seem more possible.

Sergei cocked his head. 'You are thinking about selling this shop,' he said softly.

'No—' She'd been thinking about *him*, but she couldn't deny that his pointed little questions had opened up something inside her, something she wasn't quite ready to consider. 'It was my parents' dream,' she told him. 'Their baby.'

'Weren't you their baby?'

She shook her head, wondering why he insisted on seeing everything in such a cynical light. 'You know what I mean. They poured their life savings into the shop, all their energy. My father had a stroke while stacking boxes in the stock room.' She swallowed. 'It was everything to them.'

'So it was their dream,' Sergei said quietly. 'But was it yours? You can't make someone want the same things you do.' He sounded as if he spoke from experience. 'You need to have your own dream.'

'What's your dream, then?'

'Success,' he answered shortly. 'What's yours?'

The question felt like a challenge, one Hannah didn't want to answer. Sergei gazed at her, his eyes glinting in the candlelight, the sharp angular planes of his face bathed in warm light. His was a harsh, stark beauty, yet she could not deny the whole of his features, cold and assessing as they were, worked together to make him a truly striking man. Hannah swallowed, wanting to say something light, something that would smooth over the sudden jagged sense of uncertainty Sergei had ripped open inside her. Perhaps he understood this, for he gave her a small smile and said, 'Perhaps this trip has been your dream.'

'Yes,' she said firmly. 'It was.' And it was over now. Tomorrow reality would return. In a day or two she would open the door to the shop, dusty and unused, and deal with the bills and the piles of uncatalogued merchandise and the creeping realisation that her parents' baby made very little money indeed. She had ideas, she had plans to make the shop work, and they were her plans. The shop was hers. She just didn't know if the dream was. Hannah pushed the thought away, and the resentment she couldn't help but feel that Sergei had opened up these uncertainties inside her. 'So your dream is success,' she said brightly, determined to move the focus of the conversation away from herself. 'Success in what?'

'Everything.'

'That's quite a dream.' She felt a bit shaken by his blatant arrogance, as well as the bone-deep certainty she felt in herself that such a dream was most assuredly in the reach of a man like Sergei Kholodov. 'Well, judging by this hotel you're on your way to achieving it,' she said as a waiter stepped silently into the alcove and began to serve them their starters. Sergei glanced at the young man who laid their plates on the table with a solemn concentration.

'*Spasiba*, Andrei.'

The waiter gave his boss a quick, grateful smile and then

withdrew with a little bow. Hannah felt a flicker of curiosity. Did Sergei know all his staff by name? The brochure in her room had said he employed a thousand people here. 'So how did you build this empire of yours?' she asked. 'Is it a family business?'

He stilled, staring at her for a moment, the only movement the slow rotation of his wine glass between his fingers. 'No,' he said finally. 'Not family.'

'You made it on your own?' She reached for her fork and took a bite of wafer-thin beef carpaccio.

'Yes,' Sergei said flatly. 'I learned early that is the only way you'll ever succeed. Don't depend on anyone. Don't trust anyone, either.' His voice had hardened, and his already harsh face suddenly seemed very cold.

'You must have someone you can trust,' she said after a moment. Her own life was a little lonely, but not as bad as that.

'No,' Sergei said flatly. 'No one.'

'No one who works for you?' She thought of Grigori, or even of the waiter Andrei. Both men had seemed to respect Sergei.

He lifted one shoulder in a dismissive shrug. 'I am their employer. It is a different kind of relationship.'

'A friend, then?' He didn't answer. Hannah shook her head slowly. 'I find that very sad.'

'Do you?' He sounded amused. 'I find it convenient.'

'Then that's even sadder.'

Sergei leaned forward, his eyes glittering like shards of ice or diamonds. Both cold and hard. 'At some point in your life, Hannah, you'll find out that people disappoint you. Deceive you. I find it's better to accept it and move on than let yourself continually be let down.'

'And I,' Hannah returned robustly, 'find it better to believe in people and live in hope than become as jaded and cynical as you obviously are.'

He laughed, the sound rich and deep, and leaned back in his chair. 'Well, there we are,' he said. His gaze roved over her in obvious masculine appreciation. 'Two very different people,' he murmured.

'Yes,' Hannah agreed. Her knees suddenly felt watery, her whole body shaky. The tension over their disagreement had been replaced by something else, something just as tense. And tempting.

She didn't think she was imagining the way Sergei was looking at her, his gaze roving over her so slowly, so…seductively. She certainly wasn't imagining the answering, quivering need she felt in herself, every nerve leaping to life, every sense singing to awareness. He might be cynical, but he was also sexy. Incredibly so, and her body responded to him on the most basic—and thrilling—level.

She swallowed, tried to find another topic of conversation, anything to diffuse the sudden tension that had tautened the very air between them. 'What about your parents?' she said. 'You must have depended on them, at least when you were a child.'

Sergei's eyes narrowed as his gaze snapped back to her face, his expression colder than ever. Clearly she'd picked the wrong topic. 'No,' he said. 'I'm an orphan, like you are. No family to run your little shop, and no family to run my business.'

And no family to depend on. 'When did your parents die?' she asked quietly.

'A long time ago.'

He couldn't be much more than thirty-five, she guessed. 'When you were a child?'

His eyes narrowed, lips thinning into a hard line. 'I don't know, actually. No one bothered to tell me. I was raised by my grandmother.' Hannah stared at him in surprise, and Sergei leaned forward. 'All these questions,' he mocked softly. 'You're so very curious, aren't you? Don't worry, Hannah. I survived.'

'Life is about more than survival.' Clearly he didn't like personal questions. 'In any case, I'm sorry about your parents. It must have been hard to lose them, whatever age you were.' Sergei lifted one shoulder in something like an accepting shrug, his expression completely closed.

Andrei came and cleared their plates, replacing them with the next course of *pelmeni*, a kind of Russian ravioli with minced lamb filling encased in paper-thin dough. Hannah took a bite and her eyes widened in appreciation; this was no peasant food.

Sergei noted her reaction with a faint smile, the tension that had tautened between them thankfully dissipating. 'You like it? Anatoli, the chef here, is world-famous. His signature is haute cuisine, Russian style.'

'It's delicious,' Hannah said, and took another bite. She smiled, deciding to keep the mood light. 'So you don't want to talk about your business,' she said, 'or at least anything personal.'

Sergei arched his eyebrows. 'I don't remember saying that.'

'Maybe not in so many words,' Hannah allowed, 'but I think it was pretty clear, don't you?'

He stared at her, nonplussed, and Hannah gazed evenly back. She wasn't going to let him intimidate her, not when she knew underneath all that arrogant bluster there was a kind heart. Or at least a *somewhat* kind heart. He'd looked out for her, hadn't he, in his own brusque and bossy way? She'd seen compassion in his eyes. And she trusted him, instinctively, implicitly, no matter how coldly arrogant he could seem. Underneath the bluster there was something real and good, and she felt bone-deep she was right to trust that.

His mouth twitched in something that just hinted at a smile and he set his wine glass back down on the table. 'You're very candid, aren't you?'

'If you're saying I'm honest, then yes. But not nosy,' she added, daring to tease just a little. 'If I were nosy, I'd ask you *why* you don't want to talk about personal things.'

His eyes narrowed, nostrils flaring slightly even as he smiled and picked up his wine glass once more. 'Good thing you're not nosy, then.'

Hannah watched him, curiosity sharpening inside her. Sergei Kholodov was, she decided, a man with secrets. Ones he had no intention of telling her. Yet she was intrigued and a *little* bit intimidated…and attracted. Definitely attracted. The desire she felt was heady and new, for men like Sergei Kholodov—or even men under the age of fifty—generally didn't come to Hadley Springs all that often, much less ask her out on dates. And this *was* a date…wasn't it?

'Good thing,' she finally agreed, and Sergei's mouth curved into a smile that suddenly seemed to Hannah both predatory and possessive.

'In any case,' he said, his tone turning lazy and even sensual, his gaze heavy-lidded, 'I'd much rather talk about you.'

CHAPTER THREE

'ME?' HANNAH stared at him, registering that lazy tone, that sensual smile. A thrill raced through her. 'I don't know why,' she told him. 'We've already talked about me. And I'm very boring.'

Sergei's smile deepened, his gaze sweeping slowly—so slowly—over her. 'That remains to be seen.'

She let out a little laugh. 'Trust me.'

'Let me be the judge of that.'

Hannah shrugged and gave up the argument. He'd learn soon enough how mundane her life seemed, especially to a millionaire like him. 'Okay.' She spread her hands, gave him a playfully challenging smile. 'Shoot.'

'Tell me more about this shop,' Sergei said and Hannah blinked. What had she been expecting, that he would demand to know her most intimate secrets, or lack of them? *Well, sort of.*

'I told you about it already,' she said. 'There's not much more to tell.' He said nothing, merely watched her, and so Hannah elaborated, 'It's a little shop. Just a little shop.'

'Knitting, you said?'

'Yes.'

'You like to knit?'

Hannah stared at him, swallowed. It was a logical question, an innocuous question, and yet it felt both loaded and knowing. Something about the way Sergei gazed at her with that shrewd assessment made Hannah feel as if he'd stripped away her secrets and seen right into her soul.

Which was absurd, because she didn't *have* any secrets. 'Not really,' she said, smiling. 'My mother taught me when I was little, but I never got past purling. She gave up on me eventually, much to my relief.'

'I see.' And in those two words Hannah heard how much he saw, or at least thought he saw. He really did have a dark view of the world, she decided, reading the worst into everything. He was starting to make her do that a little bit too, and she didn't like it.

'I like the business side of it,' she said, even though that wasn't quite true. *She didn't mind it* would be more accurate.

'And so you continue with this shop alone.'

'Why shouldn't I?' He was still watching her, his eyes narrowed, lips parted. Everything about him seemed sharp and hard except for those lips. They were soft, mobile, warm-looking. She was really quite fascinated with them. Hannah jerked her gaze upwards. 'I can't imagine doing anything else,' she said simply. 'And I have lots of plans to improve it.'

'It needs improving?'

'Doesn't everything? In any case, as I said before, the shop was everything to my mom and dad. I can't just let that go.'

'But to you?'

'It's very important to me,' she said firmly, but she felt, for the first time, as if she was lying. The realisation jolted her, like when you thought there was one more step on a staircase.

'Tell me about this trip of yours,' Sergei said. 'Have you been to many places?'

'A few.' She smiled, glad not to think about the shop any more. 'I bought a rail pass and have been working my way through Europe. Moscow was the last stop.'

'Which would account for the flight you missed about two hours ago.'

She swallowed, reality landing with an unwelcome thud. 'Right.'

'With my help, I don't think it should be difficult to re-schedule your flight tomorrow.'

Relief mingled with reality. Even so, as glad as she would be to have her passport sorted, she didn't want this night to end. Yet if she believed Sergei—which she did—she'd be back in Hadley Springs in twenty-four hours. 'You can pull some serious strings, I guess,' Hannah said. It was hard to imagine that kind of power.

Sergei shrugged one shoulder, the movement one of care-less and understated authority. 'In Russia it is all about who you know.'

'Well, I obviously didn't know the right people. The lady at the embassy wasn't interested in my sob story at all.' Hannah smiled wryly before quickly adding, 'She was helpful and nice, of course—'

'Of course,' Sergei agreed, his amused tone suggesting he thought otherwise. He leaned forward, eyes glinting. 'Or maybe she was just a miserable cow who never spares a thought for the hapless traveller who comes to her window.'

Hannah shook her head slowly. 'Do you think the worst of everyone?'

'I haven't thought the worst of you,' Sergei pointed out blandly.

Curious, she raised her eyebrows. 'And just what would the worst about me be?'

'That you planned to be pickpocketed in my presence so I'd help you—'

Hannah nearly choked on the wine she'd been sipping. *'What?'*

'And then finagle and flirt your way into my good graces, and most likely my bed.'

Now Hannah really did choke. She doubled over, coughing and sputtering, while Sergei solicitously poured her more water. She straightened, wiping her streaming eyes, and stared at him in disbelief. 'Do women really *do* that kind of thing? To you?'

Another one-shoulder shrug. 'On occasion.'

She shook her head, incredulous and reeling a little bit from the casual mention of his bed. And her in it. 'And they're not scared off by your incredibly surly attitude?'

Now he grinned, properly, not a lazy smile that Hannah suspected was meant to singe her senses. This was a smile of genuine humour, and she was glad. It made her grin right back. 'I wish they were,' he said.

'I'm sure,' she replied tartly. 'It must be so very tedious to fight all these women off. How do you make it down the street?'

'With difficulty.'

'Poor you.'

Still smiling, he poured her more wine. Wine she shouldn't drink, because she was already feeling rather delightfully light-headed. 'In any case, we were talking about this trip of yours. Why did you want to travel so much?'

'Because I never had before,' Hannah said simply. 'I've spent my entire life in upstate New York—'

'What about university?'

'I went to the state university, in Albany, just an hour away.'

'What did you study?'

'Literature. Poetry, mainly. Not very practical. My parents wanted me to take a degree in business.' She swallowed, remembering how they'd wrung their hands and shaken their heads. *Literature won't get you anywhere, Hannah. It won't help with the shop.*

The shop. Always the shop. The stirring of resentment surprised her. Why had she never thought this way before? Because she'd never met someone like Sergei before, asking his questions, making her doubt. And thrilling her to her very core.

'But you kept with literature?' Sergei asked, and Hannah jerked her unfocused gaze back to Sergei's knowing one.

'I left.' She shrugged, dismissing what had been a devastating decision with a simple twist of her shoulders. It was a long time ago now, and she'd never regretted it. Not really.

'Why?'

She looked up, saw that telling shrewd compassion in his narrowed gaze, and wondered how he was able to guess so much. *Know* so much. 'My father had a stroke when I was twenty. It was too difficult for my mother to cope with him and the shop, so I came home and helped out. I intended to return to school when things got settled, but somehow—'

'They never did,' Sergei finished softly, and Hannah knew he understood.

She lifted her shoulders in another accepting shrug. No point feeling sad about something that had happened years ago, something that had been her choice. 'It happens.'

'It must have been hard to leave university.'

'It was,' Hannah admitted. 'But I promised myself I'd go back, and I will one day.'

'To study business or literature?'

'Literature,' Hannah said firmly, a little surprised by how much she meant it.

Sergei's mouth curved into a smile. 'So you do have your own dream after all.'

Hannah stared at him. 'I guess I do,' she said after a moment. 'Although I'm not sure what I'd actually do with that kind of degree. I took an evening course back home, on Emily Dickinson, an American poet. But…' She shrugged, shook her head. 'It's not like I'm going to become a poet or something.'

Sergei's smile deepened. 'And here I thought you were an optimist.'

She let out a little laugh. 'Yes, I am. So who knows, maybe I'll start spouting sonnets.'

He pretended to shudder. 'Please don't.'

Hannah laughed aloud, emboldened by that little glimpse of humour. She propped her elbows on the table and hefted her wine glass aloft. '"I bring an unaccustomed wine,"' she quoted, '"To lips long parching, next to mine, And summon them to drink."'

The words fell into the stillness, created ripples in the silence like wind on the surface of a pond. The intimacy of the verse seemed to reverberate between them as Sergei's heavy-lidded gaze rested thoughtfully on her and he slowly reached for his wine glass. 'Emily Dickinson?' he surmised softly, and Hannah nodded, too affected by the lazy, languorous look in his eyes to speak. Obviously she'd had too much wine if she'd started quoting poetry. Slowly, his gaze still heavy on her, Sergei raised his glass and drank. Unable—and unwilling—to look away, Hannah drank too.

It wasn't a toast, it wasn't *anything*, and yet Hannah felt as if something inexplicably important had just passed between them, as if they'd both silently agreed…yet to what?

'How old are you now?' Sergei asked abruptly, breaking the moment, and Hannah set her wine glass down with a little clatter.

'Twenty-six. I know it's been a while since college but I will go back,' she told him with a sudden, unexpected fierceness. 'When I have the money—'

'Saved?' Sergei slotted in and she gave a little laugh.

'I know what you're thinking. I shouldn't have blown all my money on this trip if I really wanted to go back to college.' And that was probably true, but she'd *needed* this trip. After her mother had died and her closest friend Ashley had moved to California, Hannah had felt more alone than ever. She couldn't have faced continuing on, alone in the shop, struggling to make ends, if not meet, then at least see each other. She'd needed to get away, to *experience* things. Still, she knew it had been impulsive, imprudent, maybe even just plain stupid. Something a man like Sergei Kholodov never would have done.

'You probably shouldn't have,' Sergei agreed dryly. 'But sometimes a little impulsive action can be a good thing.'

Like now? For surely having dinner alone with this man was the most impulsive and maybe even imprudent thing she'd ever done. Yet Hannah knew she wouldn't trade this evening for anything. She was having too much fun.

She gave him an impish look from under her lashes. 'I'm surprised to hear you say that,' she told him, 'considering how you chewed me out this morning for leaving my passport in my pocket.'

'There's impulsive and then there's insane,' Sergei returned dryly.

'I suppose it is a fine line.'

'Very fine,' he agreed softly, and she felt the thrill of his gaze through her bones.

'So,' she said, her voice only a little bit unsteady, 'have you done anything impulsive like that? Imprudent?' She took a sip of wine, savouring the rich, velvety liquid. 'Let me guess,' she joked. 'You probably ate shoe leather and slept on the street in order to save to start your own business.'

Sergei's face darkened in an eclipse of expression, his features twisting with sudden cruel savagery, and Hannah stilled. For a second, no more, it was as if she'd had a view of the true man underneath the hard, handsome exterior, and it was someone who held darker secrets and deeper pain than she'd ever imagined. Then his face cleared and he smiled. 'You're not that far off,' he said lightly, and whatever had passed a moment before was hidden away again.

'Well, this trip was important to me,' she told him, matching his light tone. 'Whether it made sense or not.'

'So your mother called you back from university to help out. She couldn't have got someone else to help, and let you finish?'

'She gave me a choice.' She still remembered the phone call, how her mother hadn't wanted to tell her the truth about her father's condition, insisted she stay at university.

'Did she?' Sergei asked softly and Hannah stared at him. What was he suggesting? And why? He'd never even *met* her mother.

'She wanted me to finish, but I insisted on coming home,' Hannah explained. She lifted her chin and met his thoughtful gaze squarely. 'I wanted to be there.'

Sergei simply nodded, and Hannah knew he didn't believe her. She laid down her fork, her appetite—and her excitement—gone for the moment. 'What on earth has made you so cynical?' she asked. 'Everything is so suspect to you. *Everyone.*' From the boys on the street to the woman at the embassy to her very own mother. 'Why are you so—'

'Experience,' Sergei cut in succinctly.

Hannah shook her head and flung one arm out to take in their opulent surroundings. 'You're a millionaire so your life can't be all bad.'

'Don't they say money can't buy happiness?'

'Still, some things must have gone right in your life,' she insisted. 'Can't you think of one thing that's good?'

He let out a short laugh. 'You're quite the Pollyanna.'

Hannah made a face. 'That sounds kind of sappy. But if you mean am I an optimist as you said before, then yes, I'd say I am. I don't intend on going through life with a doom and gloom attitude. What good does that do you?'

Sergei stared at her for a moment. 'Well,' he finally said, 'at least it keeps you from disappointment.'

'And it keeps you from properly living as well,' Hannah returned. That was what this trip had been about: jumping in and just doing it, living life to the full. After six years of staying home, caring first for her father and then for her mother in the onset of dementia, she had been ready. She propped her elbows on the table and gave him a challenging look, eyebrows arched, lips parted. 'Tell me one really good thing that's happened to you. Or, better yet, one really good person you've known. A friend or family member. Someone who made a difference. Someone you could never be cynical about.'

'Why?' he asked and she rolled her eyes.

'Because I said so. Because I want to show you that some things—some people—are actually through-and-through good.'

He leaned forward, and Hannah saw a steely glitter in those light blue eyes that sent a shiver stealing straight down her spine. 'I could just lie.'

'Where's the fun in that?'

'Are we having fun?' he drawled softly, and Hannah gave him a playfully flirtatious look.

'Aren't we?' she said, and saw gold flare in his irises.

He held her gaze, trapped her with it, and Hannah felt her body hum with awareness, an excitement uncoiling in her middle and sending its sensual tendrils throughout her body, taking it over. It was heady, thrilling, addictive. *This* was really living…and it was something she'd never really done before. She wanted more.

'I suppose we are,' Sergei said slowly and Hannah did not look away. 'Alyona,' he finally said, abruptly, and Hannah blinked, struggling to catch up. Just gazing at him had sent her mind—and body—into a kind of hyper-aware overdrive.

'Alyona?'

'Alyona.' His neutral tone gave nothing away. 'She was one good person I knew.' And by the way he said it Hannah didn't think Alyona—whoever she was—was in his life any more.

'Well,' she said, sitting back, the heady excitement leaking out from her like air from a balloon a week after the party, 'there you go. There *is* someone good in your life. Someone you don't need to be cynical about. Tell me about her.'

'No,' he said, flatly, and Hannah stiffened a little at the rebuke, strangely hurt. She had no right to demand his secrets, even if she'd been halfway to giving him hers...the ones she hadn't even realised she had.

'Well,' she said, 'at least you have one.'

'Had.' His forbidding expression kept her from asking any more questions. She was intensely curious about this Alyona, even though Hannah knew she had no right to know. Had she been a girlfriend, a *wife*? Had Sergei loved her? Was that why he seemed so closed, so cynical now? Maybe he was hiding a broken heart. Or maybe she'd just watched too many soap operas.

'So why *are* you so suspicious of people?' she asked, trying to sound light even though she really wanted to know. 'Trusting no one?'

'I told you, experience. Most people have a reason for what they do, and it usually isn't a very nice one.' His mouth curved once more in a sensual smile. 'Except maybe you.'

'Me?'

'Yes, you. You have to be the most refreshingly—and annoyingly—optimistic person I've ever met.'

Hannah nearly sputtered in outrage. *'Annoyingly?'*

'Optimism tends to irritate us cynics.'

'Maybe you need a little more optimism in your life, then.'

Sergei considered her from heavy-lidded eyes, his gaze sweeping slowly, so slowly over her, and excitement exploded inside her. Did he *know* how sensual he looked when he gazed at her like that? Almost as if he were undressing her with his eyes. And Hannah felt awareness and desire race along her veins and nerve-endings, set her whole body to liquid flame. She wanted this. Whatever it was, whatever was going to happen, she wanted this.

His gaze flicked upwards to her face and rested there, assured, assessing. 'Maybe I do,' he murmured.

CHAPTER FOUR

WHAT the hell was he doing? Sergei watched Hannah's eyes darken—with desire, he knew—and felt that guilt needle him again. He was tired of it; since when had he had a conscience? He couldn't have done the things he'd done in this life and still keep a conscience. Yet it seemed he had, at least when it came to a woman like Hannah Pearl.

She'd reminded him of Alyona with the flashing in her eyes and the lift of the chin and the way she smiled so whimsically, as if life still offered good things. *Hope.* She'd even made him mention Alyona, and he *never* did that.

The realisation made him angry and he uncoiled himself from his chair, crossing to where Hannah waited. He held out a hand to help her rise from her seat and she took it unhesitatingly, her eyes still so heartbreakingly wide.

Did she realise how she looked? Sergei wondered. Did she have any idea of what her sweetness did to him, how it both lacerated him with guilt and filled him with need? Made him want to both believe in and shatter her illusions?

'Come.'

'Where?'

She spoke with such trust. Gently Sergei tucked a tendril of hair behind her ear. Her skin was achingly soft, and he could smell the snowdrop scent of her hair and see the pulse fluttering in her throat. 'I have a private dining room for my personal use,' he told her. 'We'll have a drink there.'

'I think I've had enough to drink,' Hannah said with a breathless little laugh.

Sergei smiled. 'Dessert, then.' She was certainly sweet enough.

Hannah stared at him, her eyes wide, and, no matter how innocent she was, Sergei knew she understood where this was leading. She bit her lip, her gaze sweeping downward for a moment and Sergei almost—almost—let her go. Told her to leave.

Forget him. Then she looked up, and he saw a new strength of determination in those violet eyes.

'Lead the way,' she said, lightly, and he threaded his fingers through hers and led her to the discreet wood-panelled door in the back of the dining room that led to his own private room.

The door snicked softly shut and he turned to her, the pretence of a drink or dessert dropped.

'What—?' she began, and then stopped, so clearly waiting.

'What am I doing?' he filled in, in a lazy murmur. 'I'm going to kiss you.'

'Kiss me—' Hannah felt a bolt of amazed longing blaze through her. She could hardly believe this was happening, that a man like Sergei—so powerful, so incredibly attractive—could want her. She stopped, let out a soft sigh that she knew was her surrender. She wanted this. This kiss, and more than that. Wherever it led. Whatever happened. She was innocent, even naive, yes, but she knew what was going on. Knew what Sergei wanted…and what she wanted. *This.*

'Kiss you,' Sergei confirmed. He reached out to cup her face, his palm rough and warm against her cheek. He let his thumb slide down to touch the fullness of her lips. 'Do you want me to kiss you?'

Hannah let out a little laugh. 'You're a man of some experience, I should think. Can't you tell?'

He laughed back, softly. 'Yes, I can tell.'

And Hannah wanted him too much to care if she seemed transparent, obvious, *eager.* She smiled, waited. She wanted this, but she still would prefer him to take the lead.

And Sergei did just that, sliding his hands under her hair, drawing her closer. She came, willingly, even as her heart thudded hard and her head fell back and she waited for the feel of his mouth on hers.

It was so easy. Too easy. Easy enough to be wrong. Sergei pushed the thought aside. He wasn't going to think about her innocence or optimism or how she made him remember. He was just going to take what was on offer, because that was what he did. That was how he'd survived.

And that was the only kind of man he could be.

He cupped her face with both of his hands, letting his thumbs slide caressingly over her jawbone, enjoying the warm, silken feel of her skin. He slid his hands along her neck, under the heavy mass of her hair, and then he drew her to him, unresisting as he'd known she would be.

The first brush of his lips against hers was exquisitely painful, because he hadn't expected to kiss her so softly, or feel it so much. Purposefully, wanting to obliterate that sweet longing and replace it with something more primal and stark, he deepened the kiss, nudging her lips further open so his tongue could slide into the moist warmth of her mouth and take sure possession.

She made a little sound, something caught between a gasp of surprise and a moan of longing, and her hands reached up to his shoulders, although whether to pull him closer or simply steady herself Sergei didn't know. Refused to care.

He'd wanted to stay rational throughout this encounter, cold-bloodedly in control, but already her innocent and unschooled response was making rational thought—or any thought—impossible, and now he deepened their kiss because he needed to, not because he was trying to prove something to her...or to himself.

His hands moved down her body, sliding over her hips, fingers slipping under the soft material of her dress. Another gasp when his hand came in contact with the bare flesh of her thigh. Her every response was artless and open; she was as honest with her body as she had been with everything else.

Sergei slid one hand around the silken length of her thigh, nudging her leg upward towards his hip, his hand sliding down to her ankle as he hooked her leg around him. He moved closer, pressing against her, his arousal—and his intent—unmistakable.

It was enough to break the moment, which, on some level, Sergei knew, was what he wanted. Even if right now his body protested with unfulfilled desire, deepening need.

He still felt the guilt.

Hannah gasped and pulled away, just a little bit. Sergei let her go. Her breath came in gasps and her lips were rosy and swollen, her hair a dark, tumbled cloud around her flushed face. She looked gorgeous.

'This...this is all going a little fast for me,' she said, and gave an unsteady laugh.

Sergei smiled. 'Is it?'

'It's wonderful,' she said, still so achingly honest and open. 'But I'm...' She pressed her hands to her face in a desperate and pointless attempt to cool the blush that scorched her cheeks. 'I'm not used to this.'

'I know that,' he told her. 'You're a virgin, aren't you?'

Hannah's eyes widened, her face flushing more, if that were even possible. She was positively crimson. 'It's obvious, I suppose,' she said, and Sergei tilted his head in acknowledgement.

'Very.'

She dropped her hands, her gaze sliding away from his as she let out a rueful little laugh that caught on its final aching note. 'You must think I'm a complete idiot.'

He could have said no. He could have drawn her into his arms and assured her that she was beautiful, desirable, perfect. All true. And then he could have taken her upstairs and made love to her all night long. In the morning she would be gone, and so would he. Easy.

Sergei said nothing.

Hannah's head was bowed, her hair falling forward in a dark swirl to hide her face. She looked young and fragile and Sergei could still taste her on his lips. He almost spoke. Then she lifted her head, her eyes darkened to the deepest violet, and took a step forward. She laid her palms flat on his chest, and he could feel the warmth of her hands through the silk of his shirt. His heart thudded hard under her palm. He stared at her, inhaled her honeyed scent, and his heart beat harder.

'I suppose,' she said softly, tilting her head back so she could look at him, her hair cascading down her back in a glinting chestnut river, 'it all depends on whether you mind.'

'Mind?' he repeated blankly. The honest, artless placement of her hands on his chest—especially when he'd just, through silence, rejected her—made him incapable of thought.

He'd never been so blindsided by a woman before, not just by her touch but by her whole self. He could see such an openness, such a willingness to be *hurt* in Hannah's eyes that it humbled and amazed and angered him all at the same time. No one should be so vulnerable. It could only lead to disappointment and pain.

'Mind me being an idiot,' she clarified in a whisper, her voice lilting and playful even though her eyes were dark and wide and he felt her fingers tremble against him. Sergei knew this needed to stop. He also knew how to do it.

'Oh, I don't mind,' he assured her in a lazy murmur, and then he closed the space between their mouths in a kiss that was nothing like the gentle embrace of a moment ago. This kiss was hard, demanding, a proof of power.

You don't move me.

He felt Hannah's yielding response and he slipped his hands from her shoulders to her hips, pulling her to him in shockingly intimate contact. At least *she* was shocked, innocent that she was, for he heard her gasp against his mouth before he deepened the kiss once more, an endless demand for her surrender.

And surrender she did, her body becoming soft and pliant, melting towards his as her mouth slackened under his onslaught and her hands came up to clench his hair. Her heart trembled against his and her breath came in mewing gasps; Sergei lost all conscious thought, blindly driven by a need that was far more than merely physical.

Why did this woman—this irritatingly optimistic Pollyanna of a woman—make him feel so much? Need so much? *Remember?*

His hands slid under her bottom and he pressed her against the door, pulling her legs around his waist, his hands rucking up her skirt. Needing to feel skin against skin. Forgetting that this was just meant to be a way to make her push him away.

Her arms locked around his neck, her head thrown back, her lips parted as her heart thundered against his. His breath came in harsh, tearing gasps, and his fingers brushed the lace of her underwear. '*Sergei,*' she said, his name a ragged whisper, and the desire and anger that had been rushing through him in a molten river of emotion so he couldn't tell one from the other froze to an icy stream of lucidity.

She was a *virgin*.

And he was mauling her against a door, her mouth swollen and maybe even bruised from his kisses.

What was he doing? What had he *done*? He'd meant to scare her off with a kiss, but *this*...willing or not, she still didn't know what she was doing.

He did.

He pushed away from her, half stumbling, a self-loathing so deep and consuming it felt like acid corroding the soul he'd thought he'd lost long ago.

'Sergei,' she said again, and this time he knew it was a question, one he couldn't answer.

He ran his hands through his hair, dragged a breath into his lungs and then let it out in a long, slow shudder. Hannah straightened, fixed her dress. Her hands trembled.

Sergei looked away. It was better this way, he knew. Better to end something he never should have begun...for both their sakes.

It wasn't supposed to go like this. She might be a virgin, innocent and optimistic as Sergei had said, but even with the most positive outlook possible Hannah knew this wasn't good. Sergei wasn't even looking at her. And after his mouth—and his hands—the places they'd been on her body, the way they'd made her *feel*—

Until now. Now she felt pretty close to wretched. She swallowed, her throat dry and aching. 'I guess I'm more of an idiot than I thought,' she finally said, trying to sound wry although her voice was little more than a croak. Still she tried to smile. She didn't know what else to do.

'Yes, you are,' Sergei returned, his voice a savage hiss. Hannah jerked back at the fury in his tone. Even though he'd just pushed her away from him, she hadn't expected it. Yet as she stood there, conscious of her tousled hair and swollen lips and rearranged clothing, her mind started to catch up to where her body had been blazing ahead. And she wondered what would have happened if Sergei hadn't stopped...and if she would have regretted it.

Even now with her clothes in disarray, her body aching, the only sound their still-ragged breathing, she didn't think she would have.

'Sergei, why—?'

'Don't.' He raked a hand through his hair once more, then dropped it to his side. 'Go to your room,' he told her, as if she were a naughty child. 'Grigori will deal with you tomorrow.'

'*Deal* with me?'

'Your passport. Your flight.' His lips curved in a grim smile. 'You can be out of this country this time tomorrow night, *milaya moya*.'

She recognised the Russian. *My sweet*. And Sergei had never sounded more cynical than when he said the endearment. 'Why did you push me away?' she asked quietly.

Sergei's nostrils flared, lips thinned. He looked so angry, yet minutes ago he'd been kissing her. Touching her. His *hands*—

'Don't, Hannah.'

'Don't what?'

'Don't be so bloody naive!' He took a step towards her, his eyes blazing. 'You want to know why I pushed you away? Because I don't do virgins, *milaya moya*, especially not ones who barely know how to kiss.'

Ouch. Hannah blinked, swallowed again, and lifted a chin. 'I don't believe—'

Sergei let out a sharp bark of laughter. 'Believe it.'

'You're just saying that,' she insisted, because Sergei was

too angry to have pushed her away out of boredom or even disgust.

His mouth twisted in a sneer. 'There's optimistic and then there's deluded. You're leaning towards the latter.'

Hannah folded her arms. Sergei's sudden rejection didn't make sense. She knew she was inexperienced, *he'd* known that, but she wasn't so naive that she hadn't felt the evidence of his desire. She'd felt it in his kiss too, in the way he'd reached for her. She'd felt the answer in herself. 'I'm not deluded.'

He arched an eyebrow, so coldly in control. 'Really?'

'Really.' Although she was starting to feel that maybe she was. She was so out of her element, beyond her experience, yet she still felt instinctively that Sergei wasn't telling the truth. He hadn't pushed her away because he'd stopped wanting her, so why?

Because he didn't want to hurt her.

The thought popped into her mind like a translucent bubble, shining and perfect. Fragile too. For if *that* wasn't a deluded thought... Sergei was surely the coldest, most cynical man she'd ever met.

Cynical about himself.

'I don't believe you,' she said slowly.

He let out a harsh laugh. 'You really are some kind of Pollyanna, always wanting to believe the best of everyone. Well, don't believe it about me—'

'You've been kind—' Hannah insisted, because she knew, deep down, it was true.

'There is no such thing as kind,' Sergei cut across her. His eyes blazed into hers, icy and hot at the same time, and full of fury. 'I said everyone has a motive, remember? And usually not a very nice one.' He took a step towards her, the action menacing. Threatening. Hannah held her ground. 'You know what my motive has been, *milaya moya*?'

'Don't call me that—'

'But you are very sweet.' He touched her cheek, lightly, and Hannah flinched. There was something ugly about his actions, his words, and she knew he was ruining it all on purpose, even if she didn't understand why. 'My motive,' he continued softly, still stroking her cheek, 'has been to get you into my bed. Why do you think I intervened with those raggedy little pickpockets? You're very beautiful, in an artless sort of way.'

Hannah swallowed. 'Your seduction technique needs a little work, then,' she told him. 'When we first met you were positively unpleasant.'

His fingers stilled for a second, no more. Then he smiled. Hannah didn't like this smile, this cruel curving of those mobile lips that was meant to convey just how coldly calculating he truly was.

'Ah, but it did work, didn't it? Taken as a whole. For I could have had you right here, against the door.' His smile widened and his eyes glittered. 'So I must have been doing something right.'

Hannah lifted her chin, ignored the lightning streak of pain his words caused to blaze through her. 'Then why did you stop?'

'Isn't it obvious?' He dropped his hand and stepped away. 'I stopped wanting you.'

Boldly, she let her gaze drop down to where the evidence of just how much he'd wanted her had pressed against her. 'Did you?' she challenged. 'I may be a virgin, Sergei, but I'm not that innocent.'

Sergei's gaze flared and narrowed. 'Admittedly, *milaya moya*, I could have taken my pleasure right here, but I am a man of more sophisticated tastes than I'm sure you've ever experienced. And frankly the effort wasn't worth the reward. Virgins are so tedious, and tend to get all emotional afterwards. I really didn't want to have to deal with your tears.'

Each word was a hammer blow, or perhaps a dagger wound, for the pain was sharp and cutting. Maybe she was deluded after all, Hannah thought numbly.

She looked up, saw Sergei watching her closely. Saw how tense he was, his body rigid, thrumming with suppressed emotion. And suddenly she knew she wasn't deluded after all. If he'd been bored by her, he'd have turned away already. Dismissed her with a drawl. He wouldn't be here, as cagey as a crouched tiger, watching, *waiting*.

She took a step forward, and now she was the one to touch his cheek. Gently, her caress a balm. 'No, Sergei,' she said softly. 'I don't believe that. You're trying to push me away and I'm not sure why. Maybe it's because you're afraid of hurting me, or maybe you're just afraid. And maybe tonight was just meant to be that—a night. I'm not quite so deluded that I think there's something more between us so quickly, but—' She swallowed, her hand resting on his cheek, felt the muscle bunch in his jaw. 'But I also know you're not telling me the truth.' She spoke out of deep instinct, and felt her own words resonate through her. She was not imagining this—

'Sergei.'

Hannah stilled as the door to the private dining room was thrown open. She turned and saw a woman stumble in. She was dressed in a stretchy black Lycra tube top and a red leather skirt that rode high on her thighs. Stiletto-heeled knee-high boots in black patent leather completed the outrageous outfit. Her hair fell nearly to her waist, tangled and peroxide-blonde, her face beautiful yet ravaged and overly made-up. She exuded cheap and blatant sexuality, and from the way she smiled at Sergei it was clear they knew each other very well.

'Sergei…' She let out a drunken giggle before speaking in Russian too slurred for Hannah even to attempt to understand.

'No,' Sergei said flatly, stepping away from Hannah, speaking English no doubt for her unhappy benefit. 'You weren't interrupting something. In fact, Varya,' he continued, his voice turning so very smooth, 'I've been expecting you.'

Hannah watched in shock as Sergei approached the woman—Varya—and snaked an arm around her waist, both steadying her and drawing her to him. She went unresistingly, naturally, curving into his solid strength as she leaned her head against his shoulder and giggled again. He murmured in Russian and she answered, her head still lolling against his shoulder, and when Sergei dropped a deliberate kiss on her forehead and drew her even closer Hannah felt her whole world come crashing down.

It was a strange feeling, surreal, just as the rest of this evening had been. Why the sight of Sergei with this woman should make her feel as if all the values and beliefs she'd built her life on were toppling Hannah couldn't yet say; all she knew was at that moment everything she'd counted on, everything she'd believed in, felt false. As if all the cynical implications Sergei had made were true, and her own optimistic assertions had been no more than the misguided sputterings of a naive schoolgirl.

She really was deluded. About everything.

'Well.' From somewhere she found her voice, croaky and hoarse as it was. 'I guess I'll leave both of you to it.'

Varya glanced at her blearily and Sergei just gave her a coolly challenging smile. 'Why don't you?' he said, and turned back to Varya.

Blindly Hannah walked from the room. One leg in front of the other, step by torturous step, until she was at the door. From behind her she heard Sergei murmur something to Varya, something that sounded loving.

Hannah paused. Something didn't feel right about this. Surely a man of such *sophisticated* tastes as Sergei would choose someone other than a worn-out-looking woman like

Varya. All of his actions had seemed so deliberate, so… *staged*.

What was happening?

Her hand still on the doorknob, she turned around. Varya's head was still lolling on Sergei's shoulder, and he gazed down at her with an expression, Hannah thought, of unbearable sadness.

Then he looked up and saw her still standing there, and his expression froze, icier than ever.

Hannah didn't know where she found the words, only that she meant them. Deeply. 'You're a better man than you think you are, Sergei.'

Something flashed across his face but was gone before Hannah could guess what it was. 'Deluded,' he drawled softly, and turned away.

Bleakly Hannah thought he must be right, and without another word she left the room.

Sergei heard the door click softly shut and let out the breath he hadn't realised he was holding.

'You're always so good to me, Sergei,' Varya mumbled in Russian, her head still on his shoulder. Her breath stank of cheap vodka. Sighing, Sergei stroked her hair.

'Have you seen Grigori?'

'I don't want him to see me like this,' Varya said, her voice ending on a hiccuppy sob. She'd always been a sentimental drunk.

'Then let's get you cleaned up.' Sergei started leading her towards the door in the back of the room that led to a private corridor. Hannah's shocked face was imprinted in his mind's eye, and the hurt and honesty in those wide violet eyes lacerated his soul with guilt and regret. Regret he couldn't afford to feel. It was better this way, he knew. He couldn't have timed Varya's entrance more perfectly. It had been a sure-fire way to rid himself of Hannah, and destroy the illusions she'd so optimistically harboured.

You're a better man than you think you are.

She really was appallingly naive.

With his arm around her he guided Varya down the corridor to a suite of rooms he kept reserved solely for her use. Varya's reappearances were fairly regular yet still unpredictable; he never knew when she was going to stumble back into his life. Still, his entire staff knew always to let her through. She had the most unrestricted access to him of any acquaintance, man or woman. They had too much history together for anything else.

Varya sat on the edge of the bed sniffling softly while Sergei ran a large bubble bath. He ordered a tray of food and fresh clothes delivered to the room and when he'd rung off Varya looked up at him with liquid eyes, mascara now streaking her cheeks.

'You're so good to me, Sergei. You should pretend you don't know me and never speak to me again.' She gave another hiccuppy sob.

Sergei smiled and sat next to her on the bed, tucking a hank of hair behind her ear. 'I could never pretend such a thing, Varya. We've known each other since we were children.'

She offered him a watery smile. 'Not much of a childhood, eh?'

'No.' Sergei observed her with a weary despair. Every time Varya drifted back into his life, she looked more worn, more *used*. The lines on her face, the caked make-up, the bloodshot eyes...all of it told a story he'd tried so hard to rewrite. Yet Varya had never wanted to take a handout, and she'd always felt ill at ease in Sergei's new world. She only came to him when she was desperate, and left as soon as she could.

'You're good to me,' Varya said again, sniffling. 'But you're so alone, Serozyha,' she continued, using her pet name for him from childhood. 'So lonely. You never let anyone close. Not even me.'

I find that very sad. 'Old habits die hard, Varya.'

She looked up at him blearily. 'I want you to be happy.'

Happy? Sergei couldn't remember the last time he'd felt such an emotion. Satisfaction, yes. Triumph, certainly. But a genuine joy? Never. 'Let's worry about you,' Sergei replied, helping her up from the bed. 'Come get in the bath.' He helped her undress, as if she were a child, knowing in her current state she couldn't do it by herself. When she finally sank beneath the bubbles and closed her eyes, Sergei left her in peace but kept the door ajar so he could check on her.

A knock sounded on the door of the suite, and after Sergei called to enter Grigori slipped into the room. His face was pale except for the port-wine birthmark that had been the reason he'd been abandoned, and had made his childhood at the orphanage a misery.

'Sergei, I'm so sorry. Security told me that Varya had been looking for you, but I didn't realise she'd found you in the restaurant—'

'It's all right,' Sergei cut off his assistant's frantic apologies. 'I'm glad she found me.'

Grigori still looked anxious, although whether for his sake or Varya's Sergei didn't know. Grigori had never told Sergei he loved Varya, but it was obvious from the naked need on his face.

'Is she—?'

'She needs a bath and a hot meal and about twelve hours' sleep,' Sergei said. Grigori nodded; they both knew Varya needed a lot more than that, just as they knew she would never take it. Life on the street had been a lot harder for her than it had been for them. A woman was far more vulnerable and those hard years had marked Varya for ever.

'And Miss Pearl...?' he asked, hesitantly, and Sergei looked away. He could still feel the softness of her hand on his cheek, the kind urgency of her words. She'd wanted to believe in him. He was glad he'd shattered at least that illusion. He turned back to Grigori.

'You can help her with her visa and passport tomorrow,' he said. 'I don't intend ever to see her again.'

CHAPTER FIVE

One year later

SERGEI stared moodily out at the Manhattan skyline as several businessmen around the conference table rustled their papers.

'Mr Kholodov…?'

Reluctantly he turned back to the table of executives, who were all eyeing him with different degrees of wary unease. He was acquiring their company, and this meeting was no more than a formality, the signing of a few papers. Clearly he was taking too long. He beckoned to the man nearest to him.

'I'm ready to sign.'

Sergei scrawled his signatures on half a dozen forms, his mind still on the city skyline.

Hadley Springs…about four hours north of New York City.

Even now, a year later, he hadn't forgotten. He hadn't forgotten a single thing about that evening. About Hannah Pearl.

He pushed the papers away, barely listening to the babble of voices as they went over the transferring of assets. What was one more company when he already had a dozen? Too restless to sit any longer, he rose from the table and walked to the floor-to-ceiling window that looked out over midtown, Central Park a green haze in the distance.

'Keep talking,' he said tersely, his back to the table. 'I'm listening.' He wasn't.

Was she the same? he wondered. As naive and optimistic and unspoiled as she'd been that night?

You're a better man than you think you are.

Or maybe life had finally taught her something, helped her to grow a necessarily calloused and cynical hide. Maybe he had. The thought gave him a little pang of loss, as absurd an emotion as that was. Everyone needed to toughen up. How else did you survive?

'Mr Kholodov…'

Did she still have her shop? It had seemed a lonely life, toiling away in a little shop she didn't seem to really like all by herself. She didn't even like knitting. Yet she'd kept at it, out of loyalty to her parents, and maybe a misplaced optimism that she could make it work. He knew enough about business to have assessed in a second that struggling little shops in the middle of nowhere didn't last long.

Had she moved, then? Found a life for herself somewhere else? Who knew, maybe she'd gone back to school. Maybe she was married.

I wouldn't even know where to go.

Amazing, Sergei thought distantly, how much he remembered. How much he still thought about her, even when he tried not to. Amazing how one night had made such a difference.

Several months after Hannah had left—Grigori had made sure she had her documents and a first-class plane ticket—Sergei had done something he'd never, ever considered doing before.

He'd contacted a private investigator, and issued instructions for the man to make initial inquiries about Alyona. About finally finding her. He hadn't seen her in over twenty years…since she was four years old, and he fourteen, both of them already weary of life.

Now the investigator was still trying to follow up various leads. The records at the orphanage had been spotty and sometimes plain wrong. And twice Sergei had told him to stop, because he wasn't sure he wanted to know. Then he'd thought of Hannah, of her guileless smile.

Tell me one really good thing that's happened to you. Or, better yet, one really good person... Someone who made a difference.

And he'd ordered the man to start his inquiries again. Maybe he did, after all these years, want to believe. Believe as Hannah did, in something—someone—good.

You have to be the most refreshingly—and annoyingly— optimistic person I've ever met.

It was annoying, Sergei reflected, that he couldn't seem to get her out of his head. Even now it made him angry.

'Mr Kholodov...'

Finally Sergei turned from the window, focused on the dozen executives waiting for him. He hadn't been listening at all.

'Fine,' he said brusquely, and they all nodded in relief. He had no idea what he'd just agreed to, but it hardly mattered. He'd signed the papers.

He turned back to the window. Hadley Springs was just four hours away. It would only be a matter of minutes on the internet to determine if she still lived there, and what her address was. And if she did...he could hire a car and be there this afternoon.

The thought shocked him, even though it felt right. Amazingly right. He could see her again, finally satisfy his curiosity—and more than that. The attraction that had exploded between them was real, and if it was finally satisfied he could get her out of his head. Forget her completely.

Wasn't that what he wanted?

Or did he just want to see her again, and never mind the reason?

It didn't matter. He'd always been a man of action, and now he knew his course. He turned back to the men assembled at the table, waiting on his word.

'I believe we're finished here, gentlemen.'

The bell on the front door to Knit & Pearl jingled merrily and Hannah looked up from her rather grim perusal of the account books. 'Hi, Lisa.'

The older woman smiled in return and placed a carrier bag of hand-knit sweaters on the counter. 'How's it looking?' she said with a nod to the books.

Hannah grimaced. 'Not good.' Lisa nodded in sympathy and, smiling, Hannah closed the book and nodded towards the bag. 'You brought some more sweaters?'

'And some hat and mitten sets. I know it's nearly spring, but it's still chilly and some people like to do their Christmas shopping early.'

'Great.' Hannah rose to look through the merchandise. Lisa Leyland had become a great friend over the last year. She'd sailed into the empty shop one chilly spring morning, several weeks after Hannah had returned from Moscow and had been feeling particularly low. After her husband had been made redundant, Lisa had needed some creative sources of income, and she'd suggested to Hannah that she sell her hand-knit sweaters through the shop and take a fifty-per-cent cut; they were some of the most popular items that Hannah had ever sold. A few months after that Lisa offered to run knitting classes in the evenings, which had brought in a little more business.

Still, none of it was enough to keep the shop afloat, a con-clusion Hannah had been drawing steadily over the last few months. No wonder her parents had racked up such huge bills, she'd realised dismally. The shop had never been a going concern, and her little improvements—the ones she could afford—weren't making much of a difference.

She refolded the last of the sweaters and put them to one side for pricing. 'These are beautiful, Lisa.'

Lisa nodded her thanks before gesturing once again to the account books lying on the counter. 'What are you going to do?' she asked quietly.

Hannah sighed and rubbed her forehead. She felt the beginnings of a headache and an incredible weariness in every joint and muscle. She'd been trying to make this shop work for so long—certainly the last year, and sometimes it felt like her whole life. And she wasn't sure she could do it any more. She knew she didn't want to.

'Keep going as long as I can, I suppose,' she said to Lisa. 'I don't know what else I can do.'

'You could sell it.'

Hannah stilled. This wasn't the first time they'd talked about this issue, but it was the first time Lisa had said it so directly. Sell the shop. Give up on everything her parents had done, had believed in…or at least she'd thought they believed in.

Since returning from Russia, she'd sometimes wondered. The things Sergei Kholodov had made her question, the discovery of their deceit she'd made upon her return…they'd changed her. Perhaps for ever.

'I'm not ready to sell it,' she told Lisa. 'I'm not even sure there's a buyer.'

'You don't know until you try.'

Hannah shook her head. She wasn't ready to think like that. This shop—just as she'd once told Sergei—had been everything to her parents, and it was all she had left of them now. Letting it go made her feel both sad and scared—and guilty, because part of her desperately wanted to do it.

I don't even know where I would go.

Funny, and strange, that it had all started with Sergei. Even now she tried not to think of him, but she just couldn't help herself. He slipped into her thoughts, under her defences. With a few pointed observations—and a devastating kiss— he'd set her doubts in motion. They'd toppled her certainties like dominoes, one after the other, creating an inevitable and depressing chain reaction until her whole world felt flattened and empty.

Now she wasn't certain of anything any more. She wasn't annoyingly optimistic either. Not that he would care. Not that he'd ever given her a thought this last year.

I don't do virgins...especially not ones who barely know how to kiss.

Even now the memory made Hannah cringe. What had she been thinking, telling him she didn't believe him? Insisting he wanted her? The memory could still make her flush with humiliation. She'd had a lot of certainties ripped away from her, starting with the most basic: that Sergei had been inter- ested in her at all.

Forcing her mind away from the memories, she turned to Lisa with as cheerful a smile as she could muster. 'Anyway, you shouldn't be telling me to sell! This is your livelihood too, you know.'

Lisa smiled wryly. 'I'm hardly making millions selling a few sweaters, Hannah. And I want to see you happy.'

'I am happy.' The response was automatic, instinctive, and also a lie. She wasn't happy. Not the way she'd once been, or at least thought she'd been. *Annoyingly optimistic.* She won- dered if she even knew how to be that kind of happy again, if such a thing were possible.

Or maybe she'd just grown up.

'I should go,' Lisa said as she buttoned up her coat once more. 'Dave has a job interview this afternoon and I want to be home when he gets back.'

'I hope it went well.' Lisa's husband had been on several job interviews, and none of them had panned out yet. They'd been surviving on Lisa's income and what temporary work Dave could get.

'Hope springs eternal,' Lisa said with a smile. She laid a comforting hand on Hannah's shoulder. 'Take care of yourself, sweetie. And think about it.'

Hannah just nodded, her gaze sliding away from Lisa because she knew her friend saw too much. She didn't want to make promises she couldn't keep, wasn't ready even to think about. She couldn't sell the shop. Even the thought still felt like a betrayal.

You are thinking about selling this shop. You need to have your own dream.

Hannah let out a groan of frustration, annoyed at herself for still thinking about Sergei Kholodov. Still remembering just about every word he'd said. It had been over a year since the night they'd had dinner, since they'd kissed. A kiss she couldn't forget, a kiss that lived on in her dreams and left her restless, awakened by aching and unfulfilled desire.

She shoved the account books into a drawer, determined to think about it later. *But when?* The question was a near-constant refrain. For the last year she'd been focused on keeping the shop afloat, trying what new initiatives and merchandise she could afford, but nothing was enough. The mortgage on the shop and house were paid, and she made enough to live a frugal, meagre existence, but that was all the income from the shop provided. One bad season, an unforeseen repair or accident...bankruptcy and destitution hovered just a breath away.

The string of bells on the door jingled again, and Hannah turned with a ready if rather weary smile for a customer. She felt the smile freeze on her face as she took in the dark-suited figure standing so incongruously in the doorway of the cosy craft shop.

It was Sergei.

She was the same. Exactly the same. Sergei felt a fierce rush of something close to joy—mingled with relief—at the sight of Hannah standing there, her hair tousled about her face, the sunlight catching its glinting strands, her eyes as wide and violet as he remembered. Smiling. Always smiling. Perhaps she was actually glad to see him.

After Grigori had done some digging and confirmed that Hannah still lived in Hadley Springs, still had her little shop, Sergei had hired a car and driven all afternoon to get here. He'd cruised down the one main street, noticing the dilapidated diner, the for-rent signs in blank-faced shop windows. The only stores doing a decent business were a discount warehouse and a garage that sold tractor parts. And Hannah's shop. No wonder it was struggling. Housed in an old weathered barn on the edge of the tiny town, the paint was flaking, the sign barely discernible. Inside it was a little better, with cubbyholes filled with bright wool and stacks of sweaters, but Hadley Springs was hardly a tourist spot. It was small and shabby and depressing and even though he was glad—too glad—to see her, Sergei was half amazed that Hannah was still here.

'Hello, Hannah.'

Sergei watched the smile slide off her face and he felt a jolt because he recognised the blankness that replaced it, that careful ironing out of expression. He did it himself all the time, had ever since he'd been a child and realised that tears and laughter both earned punishment. Better to be silent. Better not to reveal a single thing.

Yet he hadn't expected it from Hannah.

'What are you—?' She paused, moistened her lips—just

as rose-pink as he remembered—and started again. 'What are you doing here?'

He smiled faintly. 'Well, I didn't come to see the sights, I can assure you.' She still looked blank so he clarified, 'I came to see you.'

'To see me,' Hannah repeated. At first Sergei thought Hannah sounded incredulous, which he could understand, but then she let out a hollow laugh and with another jolt of shock he realised she sounded like him. She sounded cynical.

Perhaps she had changed after all.

Hannah stared at Sergei in disbelief, half expecting him to disappear, like a mirage or an impostor. Maybe a ghost. He couldn't be real. He couldn't be here, having come all the way from Russia just to see her?

It was impossible. Ridiculous. *Real.* He was here, and he was still staring at her, smiling faintly, waiting.

For what?

Her mind spun, unable to fathom why. The memory of the derisive, dismissive smile he'd given her as he'd put his arm around that woman—Varya—was still frozen in her brain. In her heart. He'd tired of her, just as he'd said. He'd wanted her gone. So why on earth had he come and found her?

She lifted her chin, regarding him coolly. 'What do you want?'

'I told you, to see you.'

'Why?'

He paused, his head cocked, his gaze sweeping slowly over her. Something flickered across his face, a dark emotion Hannah couldn't identify, and then his face cleared. Blanked. 'I wanted to see if you were the same.'

'The same?' Hannah repeated sharply. 'What do you mean? I'm a year older, in any case.' She turned away from him to fold yet again the sweaters Lisa had dropped off. Her hands trembled.

'And a year wiser, perhaps.'

She let out a sharp bark of a laugh. 'If you mean am I still annoyingly optimistic, then no, I'm not.'

His breath came out in a soft sigh. Hannah didn't turn around. 'Refreshingly optimistic, I also said.'

'It hardly matters.' She pressed her hands down hard on the soft pile of sweaters in a desperate bid to stop their trembling. Why did he affect her so much? *Still?* They'd had one evening together. One kiss. She should barely remember his name.

Sergei who?

The thought was laughable. When he'd come into the shop, despite the shock that had raced through her, another part of her had felt as if she'd been *waiting* for him to come. Had remembered exactly the piercing blue of his eyes, the hard line of his jaw. The feel of his lips.

'So.' She turned around, her hands laced together, fingers wrapped around knuckles as hard as she could. 'Satisfied?'

'Not in the least.'

She shook her head slowly. 'I have no idea why you're here, Sergei.'

He gave her a rueful smile, a smile that was soft and strangely gentle, and so at odds with the man she remembered, the man she had convinced herself in the last year was only cold. Calculating. Cruel. 'I don't know, either.'

'Well, then.' She drew in a ragged breath. 'Maybe you should just go.'

'Go? I just drove four hours to get here, Hannah. I'm not leaving quite that quickly. And,' he added, his voice dropping to a husky murmur she remembered far too well, 'I don't think you want me to.'

'You don't know anything about me.'

'Are you sure about that?' The words were a lazy challenge.

'I'm quite sure. A lot has happened to me in the last year, Sergei. I might have seemed rather simple and naive when we had dinner in Moscow, but I'm very different now, and I really can't imagine why you're here or what you want.'

'Why are you so angry?'

'*Why?*' She stared at him. 'You really need to ask? After—after the way you treated me? Made me feel?'

'It was a year ago, Hannah.'

'And when you waltz back into my life it brings it all back.'

'You see,' Sergei said, stepping closer, close enough for her to breathe in the tangy scent of his aftershave, 'I have this theory.'

She planted her fists on her hips and gave him as scathing a look as she could muster. 'Oh, really?'

'Really. And it goes like this.'

'I don't recall asking to hear your theory.'

He smiled faintly, and she felt that singeing bolt of awareness. Still. Her response to him had been—and clearly still was—impossible to ignore or deny. 'Humour me,' he said softly, and too weary—as well as a tiny bit curious—to argue, Hannah just shrugged. 'It goes like this,' he repeated, taking a step closer to her. Hannah forced herself not to move. 'You're angry because you're still affected. If you'd forgotten me, as you surely should have done, you wouldn't be looking at me now as if you'd like to carve my heart out with a teaspoon.'

Her lips twitched in something close to a smile despite her determination to stay angry and in control. 'I would, rather,' she said. Her heart had started thudding in response to his words…and the truth they held.

He smiled, that mobile mouth she remembered so well curving in sensual triumph. 'So you are affected.'

'Only according to your outrageous theory.'

'Oh, it's not just my theory,' Sergei told her softly. He'd stepped even closer now, only a hand-span away, so not only could she breathe in the scent of him but she could feel his heat. Remember his touch. 'I have evidence,' he continued in no more than a whisper, and with one finger he touched the pulse that fluttered wildly in her throat. And if that wasn't evidence enough, her indrawn breath, a gasp of shock—or was it pleasure?—damned her all the more.

Colour flamed in her face and she wished she had the strength to say something cutting, or at least step away. The trouble was, it felt too good to be standing so near him. And the single touch of his finger on her skin sent her body spinning into sensual remembrance.

'The thing is,' Sergei continued, his finger lightly stroking the column of her throat, 'I'm affected as well.'

Hannah shook her head, a matter of instinct. 'No, you aren't. You weren't. I don't know why you came here, Sergei, but—' She dragged in a desperate breath and finally stepped away. 'Surely you've satisfied your curiosity by now.'

He let his hand fall, his gaze resting on her thoughtfully. 'Not even close.'

'What do you want, then?' she demanded, and heard the ragged note in her voice. She couldn't hide anything.

'To have dinner with you.'

'Dinner?'

He raised his eyebrows. 'A meal? Food? Wine?'

And memories of another meal. Another night. Hannah knew she should shake her head, but somehow she couldn't. She could only stare. Sergei smiled. 'There must be a half-decent restaurant in this area.'

'Half-decent, maybe,' Hannah allowed, and his smile widened.

'Show me?'

He made it a question, and, despite her absolute intention to say a sane and self-respecting no, Hannah opened her mouth and said something else instead. Something she could not keep herself from saying—and feeling—even as her mind hammered out a desperate protest.

'All right.'

CHAPTER SIX

SERGEI gazed at Hannah over the rim of his wine glass. She really looked rather cross. Her eyes were shadowed, her mouth a set line. No ready smile for him, or anyone, now. He wondered what her life had been like in the last year and just how she had changed.

Hannah took a sip of wine and gazed around the restaurant—looking anywhere, it seemed, but at him. Sergei had rung Grigori to find him the most exclusive restaurant in the area, and the result was a cosy country hotel twenty miles from Hadley Springs. While he'd been dealing with directions Hannah had gone back to her house—a shabby little place behind the shop—and changed.

Now she wore a plain black dress that, to Sergei's eye, resembled a bin bag. She'd left her hair in a ponytail, her face free of make-up. Clearly she was trying to tell him something.

It didn't matter. Her body—and his—was telling him something different. And he intended to make full use of that knowledge. *That* was why he was here. The only reason he'd allow himself.

'So,' he said, taking a sip of his wine, 'tell me what you've been up to this last year.'

Hannah turned back to him in blatant disbelief. 'You really want to know?'

'I wouldn't ask otherwise.' He tried to keep the edge from

his voice. He really didn't feel like bickering. If Hannah continued to be so hostile, it would make for an arduous evening. Yet didn't he deserve it? He'd pushed her away on purpose, been deliberately cruel. Why should she welcome him now? Sergei stared broodingly into his wine, wishing he could stop feeling guilty. Stop feeling as if he actually *cared*. What the hell was he doing here?

Hannah shook her head slowly. This meal was proving to be just as surreal as the last one with Sergei had been. Then she'd been full of excitement and hope; she'd felt as if she were filled with bubbles. Now she felt flat.

'What have I been doing this last year?' she repeated slowly. 'What you'd expect. Working. Paying bills. Trying to keep body and soul together.'

'Have you taken any poetry courses?' Sergei asked, and she stared at him for a moment before answering.

'No,' she said flatly. There had been no money. No time. No *reason*. Sergei toyed with his wine glass, his gaze seeming to rest on the ruby liquid glinting within. Their starters arrived, and Hannah stared down at the artfully arranged melon slices, her appetite vanished. 'Why are you really here, Sergei?' she asked quietly. 'What do you want?'

He didn't answer for a long moment, long enough for Hannah to look up and see a surprising bleakness in those penetratingly blue eyes. 'I wanted to see you again,' he said, and Hannah had the feeling he was being more honest than he wanted or even meant to be.

She arched her eyebrows. 'You didn't give that impression the last time I saw you.'

His eyes narrowed, lips thinning. 'There is still something between us, *milaya moya*.'

'Don't call me that,' she snapped. A whole year, and yet the memories still hurt. They made her want to lash out.

'Can you deny it?'

'You certainly did,' she replied. 'You told me quite clearly that you'd lost interest and I wasn't worth the effort the last time we shared a meal.' She smiled, no more than a mirthless curving of her lips. 'Remember? You don't do virgins, Sergei. Especially ones who barely know how to kiss.' She reached for her wine glass and took a large sip. 'Fortunately,' she said, her voice spiking, 'that's not an issue any more.'

She saw Sergei's long, tapered fingers tighten around the wine glass and felt a shaft of savage satisfaction—and a pang of loss. She half wished she hadn't shared so much information, even though she was glad he knew. Surely that proved she'd moved on, even if her one attempt at a relationship had been an unmitigated disaster. Just thinking of Matthew caused a tremor of humiliated pain to rack her body.

'What a relief,' he finally said, his voice light, his eyes veiled. He turned to his starter and they didn't speak for several minutes.

Hannah felt the pressure build within her, rising up, making her want to say something. *Do* something. It was so strange and infuriating to see Sergei here, to be sitting here across from him just as before, to know he'd travelled all the way to Hadley Springs to see her...*why*?

And then of course she knew. It was obvious. Why else would a man like Sergei—powerful, *sensual*—come all this way? Just to *see* her?

Of course not. No, he must want to finish what he'd started a year ago. There *had* been something between them, something powerfully passionate, and, just as he'd said, it was still there now. She could not deny its magnetic, sensual tug, as much as it aggravated her.

Sergei looked up from his meal. 'So you've kept your parents' shop going,' he remarked mildly.

'Barely.' She felt like being honest, even if it hurt. 'I'll have to sell it or close it eventually.'

'It's not making money?'

'What do you think?' She gave a short, humourless laugh. 'It's in the middle of nowhere. Tourists drive through Hadley Springs, but they don't often stop.'

'And locals?'

'Hardly provide enough business to keep it going.'

'So how have you kept it going?' Sergei asked and Hannah shrugged.

'By cutting my own expenses. I also worked nights at a local diner, but they had to let me go. No business does well here, frankly.'

'Then leave.'

'It's not that simple.'

'It could be.'

She stared at him, eyes narrowed. 'Why do you care?'

He had started to lift one powerful shoulder in the kind of dismissive shrug only a man with his authority and wealth could give, and then stopped. Stared back. 'I don't know,' he said quietly, and a lightning bolt of longing blazed through her.

She still wanted him. Desperately. No matter what had happened before. She wanted to feel his lips on hers, his body on hers. She wanted it just as much—or maybe even more—than she had a year ago. *And if he wanted her back...*

Hannah reached for her wine, her mind spinning crazily. For surely it was crazy to actually consider finishing what they'd begun before. Yet even so the thought had slid into her mind, sly, seductive. One kiss...one night. And then *she* could be the one to walk away.

'What are you thinking?' Sergei asked, his voice husky, and Hannah jerked her startled gaze up to meet his own hooded one. He was leaning forward, his expression intent.

'Why…why do you ask?'

'Because your cheeks have turned pink and your pupils are so dilated they look black,' Sergei informed her softly. 'So naturally I wonder.'

Naturally. She imagined telling him the truth. *I'm thinking of sleeping with you.* What would he do? Would he smile? Laugh? Maybe she had this all wrong—again—and she'd be rejected for a second time.

Third, if she counted Matthew, although his rejection had been the least of her humiliations there.

'You can keep wondering,' she informed him, and kept her voice light enough that he might think she was flirting. Was she?

What was she *doing*?

Sergei stared back, saying nothing. Then he reached for the wine bottle and topped up both their glasses. 'So,' he said after a moment, his voice thoughtful, 'you've also been doing something other than working in the shop this last year.'

'Eating and sleeping.'

'And making love,' he finished softly, and she saw a flare of cobalt in those blue eyes of his that made her wonder if he was actually jealous.

Love. There had been no love with Matthew. No love, no respect, no joy. And she had no intention of telling Sergei any of that. 'Eat, drink, and be merry,' she quipped, but it fell flat for Sergei's eyes just narrowed. Dangerously. Hannah laid down her fork. She didn't want to think about Matthew, but she couldn't stand Sergei's apparent double standard either. 'You can't be *jealous*. You said you didn't even like virgins. And you've probably slept with a hundred women in the last year.'

'Hardly a hundred.'

She kept her gaze even, a challenge. 'I'm not going to quibble over numbers.'

He inclined his head in acknowledgement, but Hannah saw he still looked annoyed. Maybe even angry. She picked up her fork again and stabbed a slice of melon. 'So is this just some kind of typically Neanderthal behaviour? "I don't want her, but no one else can have her?"'

Sergei's breath came out in a soft hiss. 'I never said I didn't want you.'

Her mouth dropped open and she snapped it shut. 'Yes, you did. Quite clearly. In fact, I happen to remember the exact words.' She paused, her throat suddenly tight, aching. '"Isn't it obvious?"' she quoted. '"I stopped wanting you."'

Sergei said nothing for a moment, his assessing gaze sweeping over her. 'I started again,' he finally said, his jaw tight, and Hannah gave a harsh laugh.

'Well, thanks very much. Too bad *I* don't want *you.*'

She might as well have slapped his face. Issued a direct and insulting challenge to his masculinity. Sergei leaned forward, his eyes glittering like cold sapphires.

'Yes,' he said, 'you do.'

And Hannah couldn't deny it. How could she, when her heart beat hard and warmth flooded through her limbs in a honeyed river and she'd just—crazily—considered sleeping with him? Still was?

And he knew it.

'You want me,' Sergei clarified silkily, 'and I want you. Simple.'

Hannah stared at him. Simple? There was nothing simple about it—and yet why *shouldn't* it be simple? Why shouldn't she sleep with him? She had no more illusions about love, no more optimism that Sergei—or anyone else—was a better man than anyone thought. No reason to keep from doing exactly as her body wanted…to satisfy this craving.

And then do what her mind and maybe even her heart demanded. Walk away.

She could do it. She wasn't the same woman who had stared at Sergei a year ago with her heart in her eyes and practically begged him to want her. No, she was older now. Wiser. More jaded.

She smiled. Slowly. Sensually. Saw Sergei's eyes flare, pupils dilate. *Ha*. Two could play at this game. Except it didn't feel like a game, and she wasn't playing. Suddenly, it mattered too much. Maybe it always had. 'You're right,' she told him, her voice a husky murmur. 'I do want you.'

Sergei's eyes flared again, this time in surprise. Had he expected her to lie? She'd always been honest with him.

You're very candid, aren't you?

No more so than now.

'And since you've apparently started wanting me again…' she continued, stopping suggestively. And unable to suppress that stab of hurt. The stopping and starting thing wasn't great for her ego. Or her heart.

What was she doing?

'What,' Sergei asked, his voice sounding rather terse, 'are you suggesting?'

Not exactly the come-on line she'd been half hoping to hear. 'What do you think?'

Sergei leaned forward. 'Don't play games with me, Hannah.'

'Does this feel like a game to you?' she asked, her voice a thread.

'No,' he said quietly, 'it doesn't.'

Hannah swallowed. The very air seemed to hum and buzz around her. She had not expected this when she'd agreed to dinner. She hadn't let herself consider what might happen if they shared a second meal.

Sergei rose from the table in one graceful, fluid movement. Hannah stared at him. 'Where are you going?'

His eyes met hers in a blaze of challenge and desire, and he held out one hand for her to take. 'Where do you think?' he said softly. 'Upstairs.'

CHAPTER SEVEN

Upstairs.

Hannah stared at Sergei's outstretched hand, knew if she took it she would be saying yes. Yes to a single night. Yes to a meaningless, no-strings affair. At the thought something in her withered, shrivelled. Perhaps it was hope.

Yet wasn't this just what she wanted? She didn't believe in love any more; she wasn't holding out for a happy ending. Certainly not with Sergei. And still this attraction pulsed between them, a tidal wave of longing that threatened to pull her under. Why not let herself go? Just for a night? No emotional strings, no messy attachments. Just sex.

Sergei's eyes glittered. 'Scared?'

Did he think she was bluffing? *Was* she? Hannah stared right back and with her heart still thumping hard she took his hand. It was warm, dry, strong, and his fingers folded over hers as he tugged her up from her chair. *Upstairs.*

What was she doing?

Silently they walked from the restaurant. Hannah had no idea what would happen with the bill, but it hardly mattered. Her heart was thumping so hard it hurt. She could barely believe that she'd taken his hand, that she was letting him lead her past the reception desk, through the warm and welcoming lobby, up the open staircase, down a plushly carpeted hallway. She jerked to a stop in front of the last door, a brass plaque indicated this was the Adirondack Suite.

'Wait…you booked a room already? You thought…'

He turned around to face her, his hand still holding hers, his eyes glinting in the dim light, although with amusement or desire Hannah couldn't say. 'I booked myself a room. I needed somewhere to sleep tonight.'

Hannah swallowed. Didn't speak. Sergei took an old-fashioned brass key from his pocket. 'Having second thoughts?'

'No,' she said, lifting her chin. 'I just didn't like you thinking I was a sure thing.'

Sergei stared at her for a moment, the key resting in his palm. 'You've become rather cynical, haven't you?' he said finally, and he almost sounded sad.

'Realistic,' Hannah corrected, and he unlocked the door and ushered her in.

The suite was a retreat of understated elegance and luxury, from the fireplace already laid with logs to the huge four-poster piled high with pillows and a silk duvet. Sergei went to the fireplace, kneeling before it, and Hannah moved into the room. She dropped her coat on a chair and shed her heels, which had sunk so far into the deep carpet that it was hard to walk.

She stood by the window, gazing out at the darkened landscape, rolling fields that led to deep forest, all now cloaked with night. It was very quiet. So quiet she could hear the hard thud of her heart, and wondered if Sergei could hear it too, even from across the room.

'There.' He stood, and Hannah saw a fire already crackling to life in the hearth.

'That was quick,' she said, trying to smile. For some reason her lips weren't working and it felt like a grimace instead. Sergei noticed, his eyes narrowing.

'You *are* having second thoughts.'

'No,' Hannah said. 'But this is all a little…strange. I mean I don't… I haven't…' She stopped, shrugging. It was occurring to her that no matter what she had said or implied earlier, Sergei was going to realise—quite quickly—that she still had very little experience when it came to the bedroom. A few furtive encounters comprised a sad history indeed.

'I know,' he said, and she stared at him.

'What do you know?'

Now he was the one to shrug. 'That this isn't usual for you.'

She didn't know whether to be offended or gratified. 'Maybe I do this sort of thing all the time,' she said, and Sergei stepped closer to her.

'No,' he said. 'You don't.'

He took another step closer and she breathed in that tangy scent of his aftershave that she still remembered from so long ago. He reached up and tucked a tendril of hair behind one ear, the touch of his fingers to her skin electric, causing her to shiver as if he'd actually shocked her. Sergei smiled and Hannah knew there was nothing she could do to keep him from knowing how much he affected her. How much she wanted him.

She finally spoke, trying to keep her tone light. Keep this whole thing light. 'What, do you think you're special or something?'

'No,' he said, 'but you are.'

She hadn't expected that. Suddenly she felt the sting of tears behind her lids. Her emotions were see-sawing crazily, going from anger to sadness to something deeper than either, and over all of it this consuming need. 'Sergei—'

'Shh.' His hands came up to cup her face, his thumbs smoothing the line of her jawbone, his gaze steady and intent. It felt as if he were staring right into her soul. 'I never stopped,' he said softly, and then he bent his head and kissed her.

She'd expected something passionate, hard and demanding, purely physical. She'd convinced herself that that was all there was between them, all there ever could be. Yet Sergei's kiss was so very soft, his lips as gentle as a butterfly's brush against her mouth, and as sweet as nectar. How could such a cold, hard man be so achingly gentle?

She stilled under that kiss, let his lips move softly over hers, nudging her own apart. *I never stopped.* Was he telling her the truth, that he'd never stopped desiring her? This kiss felt as if he was. It was so amazingly tender, so heart-wrenchingly wonderful, so *surprising.* Her mouth opened under his and his tongue slipped inside, touching the tip of hers gently, a question.

A question she could only answer with a most resounding *yes.*

Her arms came up around him, revelling in the feel of his hard strength pressed against her. He deepened the kiss, his mouth taking such sure and yet tender possession of hers. His other hand curved around her hip and pulled her closer, moulding her body intimately to his. His mouth moved to her jaw, her throat, the tender curve of her shoulder, his tongue flicking along her skin, teasing and tempting. She gasped aloud as the sensations raced along her nerve endings, pooled inside her.

His mouth left her skin only for him to say one word. 'Please.'

Her mind spinning, her body on sensory overload, Hannah didn't realise what he was asking until he tugged her hand and led her to the bed. His eyes blazed into hers as he stood in front of her, the only sound the crackling of the flames.

With one sinuous tug he pulled the zip down the back of her dress and, already rather loose, it slithered off her shoulders and pooled at her feet. She stood there in only her bra and panties, shivering slightly despite the warmth of the fire, the heat of Sergei's gaze. She had an okay figure, but she knew it was nothing special. No huge boobs or tiny waist. And Sergei had probably been with supermodels…

Hannah swallowed. And shivered some more.

He touched her shoulder, his hand warm as it slid over her skin. 'Don't. Don't be ashamed. Or afraid.'

'I know I'm not like—'

'No,' he told her. 'You're better.'

She swallowed again. Nodded, because she believed him. Matthew had never told her she was beautiful. He'd never said much at all, because their meetings—Hannah couldn't even call them dates—had been so rushed, even furtive. And it was only later—too late—that she discovered why. To her own lasting shame and pain.

She pushed the thoughts away, not wanting to allow them to dim the perfection of what shimmered and pulsed between her and Sergei now. For this moment felt perfect…even if that was all it was or ever could be. A moment. A night.

Her hands trembled just a little bit as she lifted them to Sergei's shirt. She didn't think they were steady enough to undo his buttons. Sergei shrugged out of his blazer, tossed it to a chair. The movement was sinuously graceful, unbearably elegant. Hannah let her hands smooth the silk of his shirt over his shoulders. He had amazing shoulders, bunched with muscle, unbelievably wide. She could feel the heat of his skin through the silk.

Sergei reached behind her and pulled down the duvet. Then in one fluid movement he scooped Hannah up and laid her down gently on the bed. She lay there, watching him. His eyes had gone dark, almost navy as he gazed at her and un-buttoned his shirt so she could see—actually see—the hard beat of his heart, the desperate intake of breath. He was as physically affected as she was.

Sergei shrugged out of his shirt, and then his trousers and boxers quickly followed. Hannah stared at him, the sheer masculine power and beauty of his hard, honed body, his skin glowing in the firelight, and then she gasped in surprise for even in the flickering firelight she could see scars. Too many scars.

His body was a map of sorrows.

Sergei stilled, averting his face from her, his body tensing. 'You're shocked,' he said quietly. Flatly. As if he'd encountered such shock and perhaps even revulsion before.

Hannah shook her head. She *was* shocked, but more than that. 'Sad,' she whispered. 'For you.' She did not ask what had happened, or how Sergei had received so many different scars on his body. The small round red marks that dotted one forearm looked, she feared, like cigarette burns. There had to be at least twenty of them. A long, livid line ran from his right shoulder to his hip, ragged and red. And there were other scars, of different lengths and depths, all of them livid reminders that this man had so many secrets, had seen too much pain. No wonder he was so cynical.

Hannah opened her arms.

Sergei's face contorted, and Hannah couldn't tell what emotion held him in its painful thrall. Anger, sadness, regret? Perhaps just acceptance. He slid into bed next to her and pulled her into his arms, burying his head in her shoulder.

And Hannah knew this wasn't going to be what she'd thought. It wasn't going to be a night of passion, a simple satiation of the physical craving they'd both been feeling. At least, it wasn't going to be that for her.

Already it was more. Already it was incredibly intense, intimate, and scary in a whole new way.

She let her hands drift down Sergei's back, stroking his

skin, drawing him closer. He pulled away from her to look at her, his expression both fierce and gentle. A man of contradictions, of secrets, of sorrows. Hannah touched his cheek, and Sergei kissed her, deeply this time, obliterating thought, doubt, fear.

She kissed him back, surrendering to the feel of his mouth and hands, to the pleasure and pressure building inside her. Closed her eyes as he bent his head to her body, making her feel more treasured than ever. Her hands fisted in her hair and she twisted on the sheets, longing for more, for the release and satisfaction she knew they were both craving.

He kissed her everywhere, lips lingering, savouring as he moved his mouth over her breasts, her stomach, her thighs. She felt as if he was learning her body, memorising it and revering it at the same time. And when she could take no more she pushed him onto his back and started to learn his, letting her hands drift over the sleek skin, hard muscle. Even with the scars, he was a beautiful man, his body honed to perfection.

She saw besides the scars he also had two tattoos: a small, ornate crucifix on his chest, three little spires like those of St Basil's on the back of his shoulder. They intrigued her, made her realise how little she knew him. How much she wanted to. She laid her lips to his body, learning him the only way she could.

Sergei resisted her touch, pushing her hand away when her fingertips brushed his scar. Hannah wouldn't let him. Some deep, instinctive need made her want to touch him, not just a lover's caress, but a healing balm. Gently she ran her fingertip along the ridge of the scar on his torso. He shuddered.

'Don't—'

'Does it hurt?'

He stared at her, his expression open, more open than she'd ever seen it. He looked at her with both hunger and hope. 'No.'

She laid her lips to his scar, kissed her way across his body, gently, reverently, as if her touch could heal him. Was that what she wanted? To heal this dark, wounded man?

For this whole encounter had become so much more than she'd ever intended or even wanted it to be. She'd come upstairs with Sergei to satisfy a physical need, and prove to herself that that was all it was. And in doing so she was afraid she might have discovered the opposite.

She stilled for a moment, her lips hovering over him, the unwelcome realisation slamming into her. She didn't *want* this to be more than just a night. More than just physical. Not with a man like Sergei, a man who was hardened, cynical, secretive…

A man who had just kissed her almost—almost as if he loved her.

Impossible. It seemed she still was a little more naive than she'd thought.

Sergei must have noticed her hesitation, sensed something of the conflict in her, or perhaps he felt it himself. Suddenly he rolled over, flipping her onto her back, and after quickly protecting himself—and her—he drove into her in a single smooth stroke. Hannah gasped aloud at the exquisite, intense pleasure that rippled through her as her body accepted and enfolded his. All thoughts and fears were obliterated by sensation as he moved inside her, and what had felt like lovemaking became sex: simple, basic and elemental, both of them responding to the pleasure that built with each stroke until finally Hannah cried out, clutching him as she felt herself come apart and then together again in his arms.

Lying there, their bodies joined, their limbs entangled, their hearts beating against one another, Hannah felt a frightening sense of completion, of wholeness and happiness that she knew she couldn't afford to feel. It wasn't *real*. This was just sex. Simple sex, a basic bodily function. Hadn't Sergei made that clear?

You want me. I want you. Simple.

Except in that moment it didn't feel simple, not for her. Hannah drew in a shuddering breath, willed the emotions rocketing through her to recede. It would be simple. She would make sure of it, because Sergei wanted simple…and so did she.

Sergei rolled onto his back, his heart pounding and his eyes stinging in the aftermath of what had just happened between them. The memories of Hannah's lips on his scars made his insides clench and burn; it wasn't a pleasant feeling. He'd had plenty of reactions to the ravages his body had endured, from the cigarette burns his grandmother inflicted when he'd annoyed her to the knife wound that had been a warning from another gang on the street. Some women had been shocked, some repulsed, some secretly enthralled, thinking they were bedding a bad boy.

He'd never had a woman respond as Hannah had. But then he'd never had a woman like Hannah before. He swallowed, his hands clenching into fists against the sheet. He didn't want to feel this clench of his emotions; sex should have satisfied that. Instead he only felt more need.

Silently Hannah slid from the bed. Sergei heard the bathroom door click shut and felt a fierce relief. He didn't want to endure some kind of sentimental pillow talk, and he was glad Hannah seemed to feel the same. Yet as he lay there waiting for his heart rate to slow and Hannah stayed in the bathroom, he started to feel uneasy. Unsure. And he didn't like that at all.

He quickly disposed of the condom and then stalked to the bathroom, rapping sharply on the door. 'Are you all right?'

'I'm fine,' Hannah retorted. She sounded as annoyed as he felt, and somehow that irritated him all the more.

Refusing to question her further, to *care*, he swung away from the door and reached for his boxers. A few minutes later Hannah opened the door. Sergei turned, and to his surprise saw that she was dressed. She must have grabbed her clothes on the way into the bathroom. She even had her heels on.

'Where,' he asked in a dangerously mild voice, 'are you going?'

'Home.' She turned away from him, reaching for the coat she'd slung on a chair by the fire that had already died to a few flickering embers. *That* hadn't lasted long.

Sergei folded his arms. Tried to stare her down, but she wouldn't look at him. 'Why?'

Hannah thrust her arms into the sleeves of her coat. Her hair fell forward, obscuring her face. 'Because. I'm tired, and I want to sleep. I have to work tomorrow.'

All reasonable, all infuriating. Sergei did not want to consider why Hannah's no-nonsense approach to their night—or, really, few hours—together aggravated him. He was used to being the one who was first. First from the bed, first out of the door. Hannah had beaten him to it—twice.

'You can sleep here,' he said, keeping his voice even. 'I'll drive you in the morning.'

Hannah stopped buttoning her coat and gave him a long, level look. When he'd first met her, he'd seen so many emotions in those open, guileless eyes. Now he couldn't tell a thing. 'I don't think that's a good idea.'

He was getting tired of her telling him what to do. He took a step towards her. 'Well, I think it's a fine idea. And I have no desire to get dressed and drive you home after midnight.'

'Fine,' Hannah said evenly. 'I'll call a cab.'

Sergei nearly swore. 'No.'

Now he saw an emotion in her eyes: exasperation. 'What

is with you, Sergei? We both know what this was. We wanted to finish what was started a year ago, and so we did. Neither of us expected anything more than that.'

Sergei felt a muscle bunch in his jaw. He was practically grinding his teeth. 'I'm not finished.' She stared at him, and he saw her eyes darken with what he knew was sorrow or fear or maybe even anger. Something he didn't want to see there. 'And I don't think you're finished either, *milaya moya*.'

'I told you before, don't call me that.'

'It means my sweet—'

'I know what it means. And I know you only say it when you're trying to show how in control and tough you are, how much I must *want* you.' She glared at him, her eyes so dark they looked almost black, fury pulsating in every taut line of her slender body. 'I'm finished, okay? It was very nice, but I've had enough. I want to go home.'

Very *nice*? Sergei would have been offended if he believed her. And he would have believed her if her voice hadn't wobbled and her body hadn't shook as if she were in the grip of a fever, her eyes huge and dark in her pale face. She was lying. Why?

He stepped aside even though it cost him.

'All right. Go.'

Hannah stared at him in disbelief. Had she actually expected him to insist she stay? Imprison her here? And the fact that he wasn't sent a sliver of disappointment needling her heart. A ridiculous reaction, and just another reason to get out of here as fast as she could.

'Fine.' Maybe he had finished with her after all. She'd become tedious again. She smothered the stab of hurt that thought caused and marched towards the door.

Just as she reached for the handle Sergei moved. He slid

into the small space between her and the door, so close she could feel his body against hers, could *remember*—

'Don't—'

'Please stay, Hannah.' Gone was the gruff and imperious assassin of a man who called her *my sweet,* and with just three little words, uttered in such a low, raw voice, Hannah's determined defiance leaked right out of her.

'Don't,' she said again, softly, because she didn't have any more strength. It had taken just about all of it to roll from the bed as if she hadn't a care in the world, to dress and face him down as if she really wanted to go. As if it really had been simple. Just sex.

Sergei touched her cheek with one thumb, and Hannah closed her eyes. Why did he have to be kind now? Gentle when she wanted him to be gruff? Was this just another weapon, a way to control her? For she had no illusions about Sergei now; she couldn't afford to have them, even when he was kind. Even if he'd held her in his arms as if she were a treasure. He wasn't finished, so he'd make sure she wasn't either.

Yet here he was touching her cheek, his caress so very soft, his voice a thrum in his chest, a whisper that bridged the chasm that she had opened up between them.

'I don't want you to go.'

Hannah opened her eyes. Forced out the one question she knew she needed to ask. 'When, then?'

Sergei was silent for a long moment. His thumb stroked her cheek, softly, so softly. 'I don't know when,' he finally said, a confession.

And Hannah knew what that meant. There would be a when. At some point what burned between them now would flicker out to embers or even ashes. And then he would tell her to go.

Yet now with his body so close, his heart against hers, she

felt that sweet molten longing trickle through her and if he kissed her she knew she'd say yes. She'd say yes, *please*.

Still, a part of her had to fight. Fight him, and fight the fear and need in herself. She shook her head, silently, her eyes closed. Not much of a protest, but it was all she could manage.

'Hannah, please.'

His entreaty moved her, made her realise he wanted this as much as she did…whatever *this* was. An affair? A fling? She opened her eyes. Stared him down. 'Just what are you suggesting?'

'Come with me.'

'Where?'

'I have to go to Paris for a business event—come with me.'

Paris. Hannah felt a thrill of excitement and longing, even as she remained wary. She still didn't know just what Sergei was suggesting. Somehow she didn't picture them visiting the Eiffel Tower and the Louvre together, a happy couple on holiday. Yet still she wanted to go, and the knowledge surely damned her. 'And what am I meant to do there?'

His mouth quirked up and his expression turned lazy; he knew he had her. He knew he'd won. 'I'm sure we can think of a few things to do.'

So that was how it was going to be. Fighting the sudden, insane urge to cry, Hannah smiled back. She would go; had she really even had a choice? It didn't feel like it, not where Sergei was concerned. 'I'm sure we could.'

His smile widened, a smile of triumph, and he swept her into his arms, kissing her thoroughly. Yet even as his lips moved on hers she felt as if he were retreating from her, closing himself off. It was bizarre to be so physically close to someone and yet feel so utterly emotionally distant, as if all they'd shared before—the intensity, the intimacy—hadn't ever happened. Or at least it hadn't been real.

'It will be good,' Sergei told her, and Hannah buried her face in his neck, wishing she could ignore the tidal wave of longing that crashed over her as soon as she was in his arms again. 'We'll have fun,' he promised. Her face still hidden from him, Hannah didn't answer. Of course this was about fun. Easy, simple fun.

Nothing else. For either of them.

CHAPTER EIGHT

SERGEI put things in motion the very next day. They drove to New York, and from there took a private jet to Paris. As Hannah stepped aboard, eyeing the leather sofas and low tables, she gazed at Sergei in incredulity.

'This is yours?'

He shrugged his assent and a steward took their coats before retreating to the front of the plane.

'Don't you feel guilty using this big plane just for yourself?' she couldn't help but ask. 'Think of the fuel costs. You could just as easily travel first class.'

'I find this a necessary luxury,' Sergei told her. 'I need to get places quickly, and I also prefer the heightened security of a private plane. But don't worry. I assure you my businesses are environmentally aware.'

She put her hands on her hips, giving him a playfully challenging look. 'Well, I should hope so. You obviously have a lot of power, Sergei. You should use it for good.'

His lips twitched with amusement as he surveyed her. 'Thank you, teacher. Now would you like a tour of this private jet of mine?'

She acknowledged her own shameless curiosity with a little laugh. 'Yes, please.'

Sergei took her through the entire plane, from the cockpit where the pilot stood to attention and chatted with them both easily in English for several minutes, to the study with a walnut desk and leather chairs, to the bedroom in the back with a huge king-size bed and en-suite bathroom. The plane came with everything.

'Wow,' Hannah said as she surveyed the bedroom. 'You could basically live on this thing.'

Sergei stood in the doorway, watching her. 'Sometimes it feels like I do.'

She glanced at him, her breath catching in her chest at the sight of him and that intent, hooded look he was giving her. Even now, with Hannah knowing what would most assuredly happen between them later, he made her heart beat faster. 'Doesn't it get lonely?'

He shrugged. 'I'm used to it.'

To jetting around the world, Hannah wondered, *or to loneliness?* 'Is there any place you'd call home? A house or an apartment, I mean?'

'Yes.'

'In Moscow?'

He hesitated. 'Near there.'

Hannah decided not to press. 'Well, for a home in the sky, this is pretty amazing. I feel like I should pinch myself, because this can't be real.'

He came towards her in two strides, smiling as he pulled her easily into his arms. 'Oh, this is very real,' he murmured, and, hooking his leg around her ankles, he tripped her very neatly and gently back onto the bed.

Hannah laughed as she fell into the soft duvet, the mattress dipping as Sergei settled beside her. He bent to kiss her throat and Hannah's eyes fluttered closed.

'Very real,' he said again, and moved lower.

'Yes, but—' Her thoughts were scattered, hazy, as pleasure took over. Sergei slid his hand under her shirt. 'This isn't the only thing that's real.' She felt Sergei hesitate, his palm flat on her abdomen, and made herself continue, 'You didn't just bring me here for this, did you, Sergei?'

She felt his emotional withdrawal like a physical thing, as if the room had cooled ten degrees. Or maybe twenty. She opened her eyes, saw him staring down at her with a deep frown line between his eyes. Why had she pressed? She knew what she'd agreed to.

It was just, Hanna thought with a pang, when they got along so well and he smiled like that it made her want more. *Believe* in more.

'Did you?' she whispered even though she hadn't meant to press.

Gently Sergei traced the lines of her face with one finger. The arc of her eyebrow, the curve of her cheek. 'No,' he said quietly, 'I didn't.'

But then he rose from the bed, his back to her, and any intimacy that moment had woven was broken. 'Let's go back to the lounge,' he said. 'The plane will be taking off any moment.'

The extravagance continued in Paris. A limo waited for them at the airport, and drove them to the George V, where Sergei had booked a royal suite. Hannah walked through the elegant rooms with their amazing antiques and priceless paintings, unabashedly marvelling at everything. She stopped in front of a large-screen plasma TV, discreetly hidden behind a painting that swung back at the push of a button.

'I suppose this comes with cable?' she asked, eyebrows raised, and Sergei leaned one shoulder against the doorway, a smile tugging at his mouth.

'You have to pay extra.'

'I *knew* this place was cheap.'

He laughed aloud, and the sound touched Hannah's heart. She grinned at him. 'Actually,' he told her, 'I believe there are over three hundred channels.'

'Only three hundred?' She shook her head. 'That's rather shabby.'

'I'll make a complaint.'

'You must think me very gauche,' Hannah said, turning serious even though she kept her tone light. 'This is all so out of my experience.'

'I don't mind that.'

'Really?'

'Really. It was out of my experience too, once.'

'You're a self-made man.'

'You could say that.'

She nodded playfully towards the huge TV. 'So it's okay if I channel surf?'

'Oh, I think we can think of better things to do than watch TV,' Sergei told her, and closed the space between them. Hannah stepped into the circle of his arms, resting her cheek against his shoulder. She knew Sergei wanted to kiss her, to turn this softness into seduction. She wouldn't let him, not quite yet. For a second at least she just wanted to stay in the circle of his arms and feel the beat of his heart against her own. She gave a little sigh of happiness, and Sergei stepped away from her, sliding his BlackBerry out of his pocket. 'We should go.'

She tried to suppress the pang of disappointment his withdrawal gave her. 'Go? We just got here.'

'You have an appointment at a boutique in an hour.'

She stared at him in surprise. 'A boutique?'

'You'll be accompanying me to various functions. Based on the dress you wore to dinner the other night, I think you might need a few more things.' He didn't even look at her as he said it, and Hannah felt her fragile spirits plummet. Ridiculous, when Sergei had just told her he wanted to buy her clothes. What woman wouldn't want that?

Yet somehow the thought that he was going to outfit her

felt sordid. Wrong. As if he were buying her favours, or keeping her sweet.

She turned towards the bedroom. 'Okay. I'll just go freshen up.'

'Fine,' Sergei said, his gaze still focused on his phone. Hannah wondered if he even noticed she'd gone.

'Twirl.'

Hannah obeyed the saleswoman and twirled, the lavender skirt of the silk evening gown belling out around her.

From the sofa in the boutique's private dressing room, Sergei, his BlackBerry in one hand and a sheaf of papers on his lap, nodded and smiled. 'Perfect.' He turned back to his work and the saleswoman led Hannah back to the curtained changing area and the next gown she would slip on for Sergei's approval.

'How about this one?' The saleswoman reached for a gown that was a column of black silk, elegant and stark.

'Okay.' It was her third shopping trip in as many days and by now Hannah had stopped bothering to have an opinion about any of the clothes Sergei insisted on buying her. Since they'd arrived in Paris she felt as if he were putting her in her place and it wasn't a comfortable fit.

He'd distanced himself, made her feel like…like a mistress. What an awful thought. Yet clearly an imbalance existed in their relationship. An inequality.

Who was she kidding, Hannah thought as she slipped into the rather severe black dress. They didn't even *have* a relationship. They'd had three days of some spectacular sex and a few tender moments. That was all.

Yet she loved those moments, loved bantering with Sergei, watching those ice-blue eyes soften to sky when she made him laugh. Yet she felt as if Sergei was wearing his authority and power like a shield, armour that kept him closed off from every emotion.

Even so, those rare moments were enough to make her feel different, lighter, almost a return to the woman she'd once been. The woman who believed in hope, and happiness, and maybe even love.

No. She couldn't go there. Couldn't afford to think like that, because she knew it wasn't true. Hadn't the last year taught her anything? Matthew's deception, her parents' trickery, even Sergei himself. His brutal rejection back in Moscow still had the power to wound, and now she was only here because he wanted her to be. And when he stopped…

'Hannah?' Impatience edged Sergei's voice and Hannah took a deep breath.

'Coming.' She left the changing room, her steps awkward and mincing in the tight black column of a dress. Sergei's eyes narrowed as he took in the latest fashion.

'No.' He turned back to his BlackBerry, punched in a few numbers.

'No?' Hannah stood there, feeling ridiculous and a little bit vulnerable, hating that Sergei said no so quickly. Held so much sway.

He looked up again, and in his eyes she saw another swift assessment and dismissal of the dress, of her. 'No.'

'Of course,' the saleswoman murmured, attempting to lead her away. 'We'll try something else.'

Hannah jerked her arm away from the woman and stared at Sergei. 'Why no?'

'Because I don't like black.'

'You were dressed all in black when I first met you,' Hannah pointed out. 'You liked it well enough then.'

Sergei's eyes narrowed. 'All right,' he said, his tone clearly conveying that she was stretching his patience, 'I don't like black on you. It makes you look washed out.'

Hannah blinked. *Ouch,* even if she kind of agreed with him. She still didn't like how autocratic and distant he was being. She'd wanted to resist this whole shopping expedition, but she hadn't had the strength or a really good reason to. She was already accepting his largesse by getting on the plane, staying in the hotel, sleeping with him every night. Wasn't this all part of the package?

Yet still something about it felt wrong. Sordid and cheap, no matter how much money Sergei was shelling out. Silently she turned and went back to the dressing room.

'Perhaps something brighter…' the saleswoman murmured, ruffling through racks of clothing, but Hannah just shook her head.

'I'm done.'

The saleswoman looked alarmed; Hannah supposed Sergei's mistresses weren't meant to object to him dropping a fortune on their clothes. Yet already she was tired of playing the game. Fed up with acting like being showered with clothes and ordered around was what she wanted. The only times she'd enjoyed these last three days were the ones where she didn't feel like an expensive ornament, the moments where they had actually been real with each other. She could count them on one hand.

She slid the dress off and rummaged through the discarded gowns for the simple jeans and tee shirt she'd entered the boutique in. They weren't there. She looked up, saw the saleswoman eyeing her with obvious apprehension.

'Where are my clothes?'

'Mr Kholodov asked me to get rid of them—'

'*Rid* of them?' Without another word she stalked out of the changing room, the rings of the curtain clattering against one another as she pushed it aside.

Sergei looked up from his BlackBerry, his eyes flaring as

he took her in standing there in just her underwear. At least her bra and panties, worn as they might be, were her own.

Then the corner of his mouth quirked up in a smile and he lounged back against the sofa, his thumb still punching buttons. 'Aren't you a little cold?'

'No,' she said, hands on her hips, 'I'm not cold. I'm angry.'

'Angry?'

She raised her eyebrows. 'You know that word?'

Now his smile disappeared and he tossed his phone onto the sofa, leaning forward so Hannah could see the dangerous glitter in his eyes. 'Oh, yes,' he said softly. 'I know that word.'

'I don't want you to buy me clothes, Sergei.'

He arched an eyebrow. 'You have an objection to being clothed?'

'You know what I mean.'

'Actually, I don't.' He gazed at her levelly, staring her down, and from the ice in his eyes Hannah knew he wasn't going to try to understand what she meant, or where she was coming from. He didn't want to. And how could she explain? It wasn't just about the clothes. It was about everything, about them, and what she'd agreed to by coming with him on this trip. Just how much of her soul—and body—she felt she was selling.

She hadn't realised it would be like this. *Feel* like this.

'If you object to the gowns, forget them,' Sergei said abruptly. 'Just wear the lavender one tonight. It matches your eyes.'

And just like that she felt her fury trickle away, to her own shame. 'Tonight?'

'We are attending a charity gala.' Sergei continued, his voice gentling, 'Why don't you get dressed?'

'In what clothes? The saleswoman got rid of mine.'

'Pick whatever you want—'

'I don't want any of it.'

Sergei let out an exasperated breath. 'Most women I know don't object to my buying them a few clothes,' he finally said, his voice deliberately mild, and tears stung Hannah's eyes.

'Exactly,' she said, and, realising how limited her options were at the moment, standing as she was in the middle of the dressing room in her underwear, she turned on her heel and went back to the changing area.

Sergei let out an irritated breath and turned back to the text he'd been composing on his BlackBerry. Only now he'd forgotten what it was about.

Why was Hannah being so prickly? So difficult? He'd thought he'd been treating her, buying her a few nice things. Just as he'd said, most women—

Except Hannah wasn't like most women.

Sergei swore under his breath. He rose from the sofa and restlessly paced the confines of the dressing room. The last few days had been good, he'd thought. Simple. He knew what to do with a woman when he was taking her to Paris, wining and dining and pleasuring her until the small hours of the night. He'd been smugly satisfied to have Hannah exactly where he wanted her, in his bed, out of his mind. He'd finally reverted to his former self, efficient and distant, with a woman adorning his arm.

The realisation had relieved him...until now.

Now he felt edgy again, and restless, and annoyed by it all. By Hannah. How did she do this to him? Affect him so much? He'd been closing people out for years, ever since he was a child. Even Grigori and Varya didn't get close.

And Alyona—

Sergei put a halt to that thought. So he felt a bit restless. He'd get over it. And he'd keep Hannah exactly where he

wanted her. Maybe, he thought grimly, she needed a little reminder of just what kind of arrangement they had.

Several hours later Hannah stood in front of the full-length
mirror in the sumptuous bedroom of their royal suite. She
kept staring at her reflection because she couldn't quite believe it was her. Sergei had had two women from the hotel's
spa come up and work on her for most of the afternoon, mas-
saging, smoothing, waxing, and plucking until she felt sleek
and shiny, and looked it too. Her hair had been pulled up into
a smooth coil at the base of her neck, and expertly applied
make-up made her eyes look huge and smoky, her lips bee-
stung and dusky pink. She looked sexy, which was a revela-
tion. She'd never thought of herself as sexy before…not until
Sergei had come into her life, anyway.

She smoothed her hands down the front of the lavender
gown Sergei had asked her to wear tonight. With its halter top
and fluted skirt, the material lovingly moulded itself to her
body. A sheer gauzy wrap and a pair of amethyst-encrusted
stiletto heels completed the really rather amazing outfit.

Slowly Hannah drew in a breath and let it out again. After
her little outburst at the boutique earlier, she'd decided not to
object to Sergei's indulgences again. What was the point? This
was what was on offer, and she'd known that when she'd said
yes to him at the hotel. No matter now she might be feeling
frustrated or, worse, hurt.

'This is it,' she told her reflection. 'This is what you agreed
to.'

'Are you talking to yourself?' Sergei strolled into the bedroom, looking devastatingly attractive in black tie. He carried
a small velvet box in his hands, which he snapped open as he
stood behind Hannah, his gaze meeting hers in the mirror.

'*Krasivaya,*' he murmured, and dropped a kiss onto her
bare shoulder. *Beautiful.* 'I have something for you,' he added

as he withdrew a stunning diamond and amethyst choker from the velvet box. 'May I?'

Wordlessly Hannah nodded, and Sergei slipped the choker around her neck. It was gorgeous, but the stones were cold and their edges pricked the tender skin of her throat. Hannah swallowed, and felt the jewels constricting her neck. 'You may keep it,' Sergei said, carelessly, and Hannah almost quipped, *For services rendered?*

She held her tongue, bit her cheek. No need to spoil the moment. No point. 'Thank you,' she said after a moment, and she knew she didn't sound very grateful. Sergei's narrowed gaze met hers in the mirror.

'Do you object to jewels as well as clothes?'

She saw colour slash his cheekbones and knew he was annoyed. Maybe even hurt. No, that was just wishful thinking... wishing that Sergei's emotions were engaged, as hers insisted on being. Hannah drew in another deep breath.

'It's a very generous gift,' she finally said, and Sergei let out a short laugh.

'Very diplomatic, Hannah. You always were candid.'

He held her gaze in the mirror, his eyes like ice, and Hannah could not look away. Even though he didn't move, she felt as if he were stepping away from her yet again, for his emotional withdrawal was so evident. She touched the choker, the jewels still cold and sharp under her fingers. 'Thank you,' she said again and with a little sigh Sergei nodded and turned away.

'We need to leave in ten minutes,' he said over his shoulder and then he was gone.

Hannah gazed at her reflection once more. Her face was pale, her eyes wide and dazed. She didn't look quite so sexy any more. She looked...sad.

Impatiently she turned away from the mirror. *Stop it,* she

told herself. *Just stop it. You knew what you were getting into. If you don't like it, you can leave.*

She stilled, the possibility rippling through her. Leave. She could rip off this constraining choker, this elegant gown, and be out of here in minutes. She'd never see Sergei again.

And that, Hannah acknowledged hollowly, was why she stayed.

'Ready?' Sergei called from the suite's lounge, and reaching for her wrap—which provided no warmth—Hannah went.

An hour later she stood next to Sergei, a flute of champagne clenched in one hand, her cheeks aching from smiling as Sergei talked business with one well-heeled guest after another. Beyond the barest flicker of a glance or nod from his companions, she was ignored. Talk about feeling like an ornament.

As Sergei launched into another deep conversation— this time in French—Hannah decided to get some fresh air. Obviously she didn't need to be here, except as Sergei's accessory. She murmured her excuses—that nobody seemed to hear—and then crossed the elegant hotel ballroom, the clink of crystal and the conversation of five hundred of Paris society's darlings a cacophony of sound all around her. A wall of French doors led onto a terrace, and Hannah slipped through them with a little sigh of relief.

The spring air was warm and fragrant, the night quiet, the sound from inside no more than a distant murmur. Hannah moved to the railing that looked out over a private garden, now lost in shadows although she could smell roses and lilac. She breathed in deeply and let the peace of the night wash over her and steal through her soul. At least she tried to.

How, she wondered bleakly, could she feel so sad when she was standing on the terrace of a luxurious hotel, wearing a beautiful dress, with a gorgeous man inside who undoubtedly would take her home in a few hours and make love to her for most of the night?

She should be walking on air. Instead she felt empty.

'There you are. Sergei's latest.'

Hannah froze, then forced herself to turn around. In the darkness she could barely make out the face of the man who stood there, lounging in the doorway. She could still feel how he was studying her, his gaze arrogant as he completed an insultingly thorough sweep of her body.

'I'm afraid I don't know you,' she said stiffly. He came closer, and she saw the sardonic cast of his features; he was handsome, but his mouth was thin and cruel and his eyes were bloodshot.

'You could get to know me,' he offered in a soft drawl. 'When Sergei's done with you.'

Hannah recoiled physically from his blatantly crude suggestion. 'Excuse me,' she said coldly, and made to move past him, her legs weak and watery with the shock of such an awful encounter. He grabbed her arm, and Hannah froze again, her skin crawling at the feel of his fingers on her bare flesh.

'It's happened before, you know. I don't mind taking Sergei's leftovers.'

She shook his arm off, her body trembling with affront and even fear. 'You're disgusting.'

He laughed, the sound one of genuine amusement. 'So self-righteous. You *are* his mistress, aren't you?'

And this time Hannah froze both inside and out. Not just her body, but her heart. She stood there, as unable to move as if she were encased in ice.

His mistress. That was exactly what she was. And this clearly was how she should expect to be treated.

'Well?' the man demanded, his voice turning surly and slurred. He was clearly drunk; perhaps he wouldn't have taken such obnoxious liberties with her otherwise. Still the bleak truth of her position both in society and Sergei's life remained, unavoidable, undeniable.

'Yes,' Hannah said stiffly, 'that's exactly what I am. Sergei's mistress. Never yours.' And with her head held high and her heart still icy, she stalked past him, only to give a little scream of fear when yet another hand clamped around her wrist and someone swung her around.

She stared in shock at Sergei, his eyes blazing blue fire. 'What the *hell*,' he demanded, 'do you think you're doing?'

CHAPTER NINE

'WHAT *I'm* doing—' Hannah gasped, startled by the raw fury in Sergei's blazing gaze.

'Don't say another word. We're leaving.' He glanced beyond her to the man who still lounged, smirking, on the terrace. 'And you, de Fourney,' he said in a low growl, 'I'll deal with you later. Consider this your warning.'

The undisguised menace in Sergei's voice made Hannah shiver even as she hurried to keep up with him, his hand still clamped around her wrist.

'Sergei, what is *wrong* with you?' she demanded in a harsh whisper as he pushed through the hotel's front doors. 'Why are you so angry?'

'What were you doing with de Fourney?'

'The man on the terrace?' She jerked her arm away from him, forcing him to stop and turn to face her although he still seethed barely leashed anger. 'Are you actually so—so boneheaded to be jealous of that slimy toad?'

'I'm not *jealous*.'

'Then why are you acting like some kind of Neanderthal?' Hannah demanded. 'Dragging me back to your stupid cave?'

'I'll remind you,' he told her softly, 'my cave costs five thousand dollars a night.'

She felt as if he'd slapped her. 'Thanks for making me

feel cheaper than I already did,' she whispered, and pushed past him.

'Hannah—' He caught up with her, and a driver leapt to attention, opening the door of the limo idling by the kerb. Hannah slid inside, knowing she had no choice. What could she do? Where could she go? She was virtually Sergei's prisoner. Worse...his mistress.

She closed her eyes, wishing she could stem the wave of pain that engulfed her at the thought. Sergei slid in next to her and slammed the door.

She still didn't understand why he was angry. If he'd overheard one second of her conversation with that jerk he could hardly be jealous.

She glanced at him, saw his harsh profile, his jaw bunched so tight Hannah thought he might break a tooth. Biting her lip, she turned away and stared out of the window as the limo slid seamlessly into the traffic near the Arc de Triomphe.

They didn't speak all the way back to the hotel. The tension in the limo was heavy, thick with anger Hannah didn't fully understand. Finally as she entered the royal suite, her heels clicking on the marble floor of the elegant foyer, she confronted him. She threw her wrap onto a fragile-looking antique chaise as Sergei jerked off his tie and tossed it onto a chair.

'What,' Hannah asked, her anger a hot, hurting lump in her chest, 'do you think *you're* doing?'

He turned around, his jaw still working, his fury evident in every taut line of his muscular body. 'What were you doing, talking to that *zhopa*? Guy de Fourney?'

'Is that his name? Obviously the two of you are good friends.'

'What?' Sergei glared at her. 'He is as sleazy and corrupt as they come. I have nothing to do with him.'

'Nothing?' Hannah repeated, her voice silky despite the tremors that now racked her body. 'He indicated otherwise.'

'And you believed him?'

'Why shouldn't I? He said he's—' she swallowed, her voice hitching revealingly '—had your leftovers.'

Sergei stared at her for a long moment. Then he swore in Russian. 'That man is—' He slashed a hand through the air. 'He seeks to offend.'

'I don't know if he meant to be offensive,' Hannah replied with a lift of her chin. 'He was just stating facts, wasn't he?'

'No,' Sergei ground out, 'he wasn't.'

'So he hasn't shared a mistress of yours?'

Sergei's face darkened dangerously. '*Shared?* Of course not! What do you think—?'

She folded her arms, half wondering why she was pushing this. Did she really want to know? 'He didn't ever have sex with a woman you've had sex with?' she demanded, her voice only just level. Sergei said nothing. Silence was damning. 'See,' Hannah said softly. 'He was just speaking the truth.'

'That is not the truth!' Sergei snapped. 'Not the way he said it. And in any case I hardly keep track of the man's movements.'

'Or those of your discarded mistresses.'

He let out a low breath. 'Very well. I do believe it is possible that once a woman I— A woman went to him after she'd been with me.' His expression razored her, sharp and cutting. 'But that hardly matters—'

'Oh, no?' Hannah interjected. He was right; it didn't matter, not really. What mattered was how cheap the exchange with Guy de Fourney had made her feel. How cheap this affair made her feel.

Sergei stabbed a finger towards her. 'I have no interest in what a piece of trash like Guy de Fourney says. I care what *you* say,' he continued. For the first time since she'd met him his accent, usually faint, became so pronounced that Hannah stepped closer to understand him. 'You called yourself my mistress.'

She blinked, baffled by his remark. 'That's what I am.'

'No, it is not.' He folded his arms, still furious and maybe even—hurt? Was it possible?

'What do you intend to call me, then?' she demanded. 'You whisk me away to Paris, you buy me clothes, you have sex with me every night—' Her voice rose, all the hurt she'd been holding in tumbling from her lips. 'You buy me this—this dog collar!' With one jerk she pulled the choker from her neck, the stones cutting her skin deep enough to draw tiny droplets of blood. Hannah flung the necklace onto the floor; it landed with an expensive-sounding clatter.

'Hannah—' Her name was an inadvertent cry as Sergei stretched a hand out to her, his horrified gaze on the bloody marks on her neck.

'Isn't it all true? Isn't this what we agreed on?' Hannah demanded. She felt tears sting her eyes and she blinked them away furiously. 'Isn't this what you *want*?'

Sergei crossed to stand in front of her. He withdrew a perfectly starched handkerchief from his breast pocket and gently dabbed at the scratches on her throat. 'No,' he said quietly, 'it isn't what I want.'

Hannah closed her eyes. Tears leaked out from under her lids, and she brushed them away, impatient, embarrassed.

'I didn't mean to make you cry.' Sergei touched his thumb to her eye, her cheek, wiping away the traces of her tears. 'Please don't cry, Hannah.' His voice sounded choked. 'I cannot bear it.'

She opened her eyes, surprised and moved to see his harshly handsome face contorted in anguish. 'I'm sorry.' She drew in a ragged breath and blinked hard, forcing the lump that had risen into her throat back down. She could still feel it, hot and heavy in her chest. 'I'm sorry,' she said again, more composed now. She took a step away from him. 'I don't understand you, Sergei. You made it quite clear what you wanted back in New York. This was meant to be fun, a fling, and I accepted that. I'm trying to accept it, anyway. But even when I do you still get angry. Back at the hotel—you treated me like a—a possession! Something you can just drag around.'

The anguish had left Sergei's face, his expression wiped as clean as a slate. 'I'm sorry,' he finally said, his voice neutral. 'I didn't mean to hurt you.'

'Why were you so angry?' Hannah demanded rawly. 'When I was just stating facts? Because I *am* your mistress, aren't I? That's how all those people at the charity event tonight think of me. The ornament on your arm.' It hurt to say it, but she wanted to be clear. She wanted Sergei to know she wasn't fooled.

Sergei pressed his lips together. So much for anguish; now he just looked annoyed. 'I don't know how they think of you—'

'Don't you?'

'Fine.' He rubbed a hand over his face, then dropped it abruptly. 'Fine. Yes. They think of you as my mistress. I've never—I've never been with the same woman for very long. No one would think now that I was in a—a proper relationship.'

'And *we're* not in a proper relationship,' Hannah pointed out. 'We're not equals in this. You dress me up like a doll and parade me around and sleep with me and when you've had enough you'll send me back where I came from.' It hurt so much to say it, but she knew she had to. For her own sake as much as Sergei's. She needed the reminder of just what it was they were doing here.

'Don't,' Sergei said sharply. 'Don't make what is between us sound so—so sordid.'

'But it *is* sordid, Sergei.' It was to her, anyway. 'Like I said before, I'm just stating facts.'

His jaw tightened and he folded his arms. 'I don't like those facts.'

'Don't you?' She let out a short, disbelieving laugh. 'Because those are your facts. The rules you set down—'

'I don't remember making any rules.'

Hannah stared at him, genuinely confused. What was Sergei trying to tell her? That he *didn't* want this? The thought was surely laughable. 'Why are you arguing the point?' she asked quietly. 'Do you just not like someone spelling it out to you? Because if you've never even been in a proper relationship before, somehow I don't think you're looking to start.'

Sergei stared at her, his gaze level and yet fathomless, his mouth a hard line. 'Maybe I am,' he said at last, and despite the fierce thrill of hope that rippled through her Hannah shook her head.

'No, you're not.'

Sergei's lips curved in a grim smile. 'You're so sure about that?'

'Yes.'

'And here I thought you believed the best in everyone,' he drawled softly.

She swallowed and then hardened her resolve. 'Not any more.'

He shook his head. 'What happened to your optimism, Hannah? Because a year ago—'

'I'm not the same person I was a year ago, Sergei. And you probably aren't either.'

'No,' he agreed quietly, 'I'm not.'

She nodded, even though her insides felt leaden, weighed down with sorrow. 'People change.'

'Why did you change? What happened?' He paused, his

mouth twisting before resuming its familiar flat line. 'Was it my fault?'

'Your fault?' She shook her head slowly. 'No…although our—our evening together probably started it. I was so naive, I realise that now, and when I saw you with—with Varya—'

'It wasn't what it looked like.'

'Really?' Hannah raised her eyebrows, not understanding why Sergei felt the need to rewrite their history now. 'You certainly went to some lengths to convince me it was just what it looked like then. I remember how insistent I was that you weren't being truthful, that you—you—'

'Were a better man than I thought?' Sergei finished softly, and Hannah blinked.

'Why are you bringing this all up now?'

'Because you changed me, Hannah. In a different way than I changed you.'

'It wasn't all about you,' Hannah said quickly. 'All right, your—your rejection hurt. Obviously. But other things happened.'

'Like what?'

She shrugged. 'I came back to New York and I felt pretty low. I rushed into a relationship—and it wasn't so great.' She shrugged again, not wanting to tell him about Matthew, about the humiliation and heartache. How dirty and used it had all made her feel. By the darkening of his features she didn't think Sergei wanted to hear. 'And—and the shop had been struggling for so long,' she continued, 'and I really wanted to try to make a success of it, for my parents' sake. But…' She pressed her lips together, reluctant to reveal any more.

'But?' Sergei prompted softly.

'I started going through their things—I'd been putting it off since my mom died, but I figured it was time—anyway,' she continued hurriedly, wanting to get through it all, 'I found out some things. They weren't really honest with me.' She folded her arms, stared at the floor. 'I thought my mother was giving me a choice, to come back from college and help out, but I found some paperwork and I saw that she'd had me withdrawn even before she telephoned me. She'd already decided I wasn't coming back for the second semester, but she pretended it was my decision.' The realisation had felt like a betrayal, and it had made her angry. Uselessly so, for how could you stay angry with someone who was dead?

'Maybe,' Sergei said quietly, 'she thought she was being kind. She wanted you to feel like you had more control—'

'But it was a lie,' Hannah cut him off. 'And there were other things. Other lies. Credit card bills I didn't know about until after her death. I thought she'd hidden them away because of her dementia and didn't realise what she was doing. But they went back farther than I thought.' She drew in a deep breath and let it out slowly. 'I think both my parents were hiding from me how badly the shop had been doing because they wanted me to take it on.'

'Obviously it was important to them.'

'More important than me.' She sighed. 'I sound like a child having a tantrum, I know.'

'It never feels good to have your illusions ripped away.'

'And that's what they were,' Hannah agreed. 'Illusions.'

'Perhaps your parents were just trying to protect you.'

'Who's the optimist now?' Hannah shook her head. 'No, they were trying to trap me. Trap me into staying and running their stupid little shop when they couldn't any longer because it meant more to them than I ever did.' The words tumbled out of her, savage and surprising. Until that moment she hadn't realised she had them inside her. She felt her lips tremble, her body shake.

The words sounded so ugly, and yet she meant them. And she never would have said them or even thought them if that first evening with Sergei hadn't started her thinking.

Doubting. Yet she could hardly blame him for her parents' actions, or for the disaster of her relationship with Matthew, or her own blind naiveté.

'Come here.'

'What—?'

'Come here,' Sergei said again, gently, and then before she could move he came towards her, enfolding her in his arms. Hannah resisted at first, because Sergei had never hugged her before. Not as gently as this. An embrace of comfort, of compassion. Her throat closed up and her eyes welled yet again with tears and this time she did not blink them away. She let them slide down her face as she laid her cheek against Sergei's shoulder and breathed in the scent of his aftershave, the scent that was just him. She wept for all the loss she had felt over the years: the loss of her parents, and the loss of herself, or at least the self she had been. Standing there in the circle of his arms, she felt both safe and cared for, and it made her realise she hadn't felt like that in a long, long time.

'It can't have been easy,' Sergei said after a moment, his hands stroking her back, 'to have carried all that alone.'

'I wasn't completely alone,' Hannah protested, her voice muffled against his shoulder. 'I do have some friends, you know—'

'But you didn't want to burden them with your problems, because they had enough of their own.'

She thought of Ashley, still struggling to make a new life for herself in California, and Lisa, so anxious about her husband's job situation. 'Sort of, I suppose. How did you—?'

'I know *you*,' Sergei told her.

She didn't answer, couldn't answer, because the thought that Sergei knew her at all sent hope spinning dizzily through her once more and she was afraid of hope, afraid of the following disappointment. This was *Sergei*. Sergei Kholodov, the coldest, most cynical man she'd ever encountered. The man who was now holding her so gently.

'I'm sorry,' she said, sniffing and stepping away from him. He let her go. 'I've probably ruined your jacket.'

'Dry-cleaning does wonders.'

'Right.' She tried to smile, but it wobbled and threatened to slide right off her face. She didn't know what to do with what she'd revealed, what Sergei now knew. She hadn't meant to say all that; she'd been trying not even to think it for years.

Sergei sighed and shook his head. 'I'm sorry you went through all this. If I hadn't—'

'Don't blame yourself, Sergei,' she said, sniffing. 'Honestly, people have dealt with far worse. And it's all part of growing up, isn't it?' She tried to inject a lightness into her voice, a lightness she didn't feel. 'And at least now I'm no longer annoyingly optimistic.'

'Well, actually,' he told her with a tiny smile, 'your annoying optimism is what changed me. Made me hope—for better things. Believe that not all people are as selfish and disappointing as I thought they were.'

Hannah stared at him in disbelief. *This* she had not expected. 'And did it work?'

His smile turned wry, maybe even sad. 'I'm trying, Hannah.'

'Trying to do what?'

'To believe.' He took a step towards her, closing the space she'd just created between them. 'That's why I was so angry tonight. I didn't—I don't want you just to be my mistress. I'll admit that's how I've treated women. Dolls to keep at a distance, to enjoy and even use and then—discard.' Hannah flinched at the stark brutality of his words. He nodded in acknowledgement. 'I know. It's not pretty, is it?'

'At least you're admitting it now.'

'But you're different. At least, I'm different when I'm with you. I can be…when I let myself.'

He was speaking words she had, on some level, longed to hear, yet Hannah still stayed sceptical. Suspicious. Maybe she had become too cynical, or maybe she just wanted to protect herself. 'So I'm the first woman you've met that you didn't want to treat like a whore?'

Now Sergei flinched. 'That's not completely fair.'

Hannah gave an accepting shrug. She knew it wasn't. 'All right, a mistress, then.'

'Yes.'

She let out a shuddering breath. 'I'm not sure I even know what that means.'

'I don't either. I told you, I've never had a proper relationship before, not a romantic one. And not really one of any kind,' he added with stark honesty. 'I have employees and colleagues and acquaintances.' He shrugged, giving her a half-smile, and the icy suspicion around her heart thawed, just a little bit.

'Never? Not even one?'

'No.'

Hannah shook her head. 'Sergei, what a lonely life you've led.'

He inclined his head in acknowledgement. 'Yes. But maybe—maybe now it is time for something different.'

Her heart leapt even as she took a step backwards. 'How different? How do you change who you are?'

His face blanked, and Hannah had the feeling that she'd hurt him with her blunt question. 'I don't know,' he said quietly. 'I don't know if I *can* change.' His mouth thinned into a hard line once more, and Hannah cursed herself for her stupid remark. She could see she was losing him again; he was closing her off just as he had before, and she knew she couldn't

let that happen. Not now, when he'd b
even if she was still unsure and frankly t

'I suppose you could try,' she said, know
choice. A choice she had control over. 'We co
swallowed. 'I still—I want to believe too.'

He gazed at her, his face expressionless, and Hannah
whatever they were talking about—whatever relationsh
they could have—was held in the balance now. She held her
breath, her body tense, her heart thudding, everything inside
her straining, waiting…

'All right,' Sergei finally said. He smiled, a tiny quirking
of one corner of his mouth, although his eyes still looked dark
and shadowed. 'All right.'

Hannah let out a shaky laugh. 'So what happens now, exactly?'

'Come away with me.'

She tensed. 'Didn't we already do that? I came to Paris.'

'Come with me somewhere different,' Sergei said. His gaze
was steady on hers as he added, 'Home.'

een so open. Not now,

rrified.

ing this was a

ld try.' She

knew

ip

TEN

SERGEI stared down at the report he needed to read, facts and figures blurring before his eyes. Meaningless. He hadn't been able to concentrate on anything in the two days since he'd told Hannah he wanted something different. Something more. The trouble was, he had no idea what that was or how he went about getting it.

Sighing, he rubbed a hand over his face and pushed the papers away. He'd thought being open—for the first time in his life—would firm his resolve. Usually when he chose a course of action he had no doubts, no hesitations. Yet now he didn't know what action to take, what to *do*. What to feel.

It was a realisation that left him restless, edgy, impatient with everything. So far something more was proving to feel like something less.

A knock sounded on the door of his office and Grigori poked his head in. Sergei bid him to enter with an irritable wave of his hand.

'Some letters for you to sign,' Grigori murmured, placing a few typed pages before him. Sergei scrawled his signature, barely looking at the print. Seeming to sense something of his mood, Grigori retrieved them without a word.

'Has there been any news of Varya?' Sergei asked abruptly. Grigori shook his head. 'Maybe soon,' he said quietly. Sergei nodded, knowing that Varya's latest episode had given his assistant great worry and grief. She'd shown up at the office several weeks ago, her eye blackened and her arm in a sling. Sergei had been furious; he had wanted to force her to stay, to be *safe*, but Varya had only laughed—brittlely—and said she was fine. She could take care of herself. And she'd melted away from them again, back onto the street.

Sergei knew she was too proud to accept his charity, too afraid to live in his world. He'd known that for years, and yet it still filled him with a deep sorrow.

How do you change who you are?

Hannah's question reverberated bleakly through him. Varya did not seem able to change; the deprivations of their childhood had scarred her for life. Perhaps he was the same. Perhaps this inability to draw closer to another person was impossible to overcome. Perhaps he was too damaged, as the therapist who had assessed him at fourteen years old had said.

Perhaps he couldn't change at all.

'Sergei?'

Sergei glanced up, startled to see Grigori was still there. He'd been so lost in his gloomy thoughts he'd barely noticed the other man. 'Yes. Here.' He handed him the last of the letters and Grigori turned towards the door.

'Grigori…' Sergei said, and then stopped, because he didn't know how to go on.

'Yes, Sergei?'

'Do you…do you love Varya?' Grigori blushed, his birthmark turned an even deeper red, and said nothing. 'I'm sorry,' Sergei said. 'I did not mean to embarrass you.'

'I know,' Grigori mumbled, 'that it will come to nothing.'

Sergei rolled a gold-plated pen between his fingers, his features settled into a frown. 'Have you always loved her?'

'Since we were children,' Grigori confessed quietly. Sergei could picture them both as they'd been in the orphanage: Varya ethereally beautiful and dreamy, Grigori slight and stammering. Both easy targets. 'We made up stories about what we would do when we left the orphanage.'

Sergei stared at him in surprise, for he had never known that. Even though he'd done his best to protect Grigori and Varya both in the orphanage and on the street, he'd still always been a loner. He'd preferred it that way. 'Stories?'

Grigori gave an embarrassed little shrug. 'Yes…we were going to save our kopeks and buy a *dacha*, somewhere deep in the country, and live there together.' He smiled sadly. 'Some dreams come to nothing, eh?'

'Maybe you still could,' Sergei said, even though he knew the sentiment was hollow. 'You are both still young.'

'Ah, Serozhya,' Grigori said, 'none of us are young. We are old, and we've been old for far too long.' With another sad smile, he took the letters and left the room.

Sergei stared blindly out of the window, a weary sorrow flooding through him. He wondered if any of the children he'd grown up with had found happiness. Had Alyona? A few days ago the detective he'd hired had rung, said he had some fresh leads to follow in California. Sergei didn't let himself think about it, didn't dare hope. At least, he told himself now, Alyona had had a *chance*—

Restlessly he rose from his desk and paced the spacious confines of his office, a sumptuous cage. That morning he had left Hannah in his penthouse apartment overlooking Manege Square with his platinum credit card and instructions to buy whatever she wished, his driver at her disposal.

She'd stared at him, her expression so very neutral, the credit card resting in her open palm. 'Haven't we done this already?' she asked and Sergei had stared at her in bewilderment.

'We are going to the country. You cannot wear ball gowns.' She'd said nothing, but he'd sensed her disappointment and it frustrated and even angered him.

'You can choose whatever you like, but you need something to wear, Hannah.' She still hadn't spoken, only looked sad, and in irritation he'd snapped, 'Or don't buy anything if you don't wish to. Sit here and sulk all morning.' And knowing he was the one who sounded childish, he'd slammed out of the apartment.

Now as he prowled his office the memory embarrassed and angered him. This was not what he'd meant when he told Hannah he wanted something different. Yet he felt paralysed to do anything about it, unable even to begin to know *how* to change, and that frustrated him all the more.

Perhaps, Sergei considered bleakly, as he stopped pacing to stare out of the window at the grey city streets below, change was impossible.

Perhaps *they* were impossible. Perhaps pursuing a relationship with Hannah was a fool's errand. A hopeless cause…just as he had been.

Hannah knew the morning hadn't gone well. She wasn't exactly sure how it happened, only that some time between Sergei telling her he had to work and handing her his credit card she'd felt her tender bloom of hope wither at the root. When he'd slammed out of the apartment, leaving her quite alone, she'd been shocked and also sorry, because she had the feeling she'd hurt Sergei even though he would never admit as much.

There were a lot of things he might never do, she reflected. A lot of ways he might never change. In the two days since that allegedly transforming conversation in Paris, they'd both tiptoed around each other, awkward and hesitant, like actors who didn't know their lines. The sex was still fine; the sex was spectacular. But relationships could not be conducted solely in bed.

And as for what happened out of it…Hannah had no idea

if that would ever work. She certainly knew it wasn't working now.

Half an hour after Sergei stormed out of the apartment his driver showed up to take her around town in a luxury bulletproof sedan with tinted windows and a souped-up engine. Hannah had balked a little bit at the car, and the driver, a surly-looking man with a wicked-looking scar bisecting his right cheek, smiled grimly and said, 'Mr Kholodov takes no risks.'

Good grief, Hannah thought as she slid inside, what kind of business was Sergei *in*? Driving around Moscow in that gangster's car made her feel as if she didn't know him at all.

Throughout the morning as she selected a small variety of practical clothes—nothing fancy, nothing sexy—she considered just what she did know of Sergei. She knew he was rich. She knew he was ruthless. She knew he could be kind. As for actual *facts*...she knew he was an orphan, raised by his grandmother, and that he had scars all over his body. And two tattoos. She didn't know how he'd come by those scars—or tattoos—or why there was no one in his life he'd ever felt he could trust or love. She didn't know who Alyona was, or where she'd gone.

There was a lot, Hannah decided dispiritedly, that she didn't know. And she had a feeling Sergei had no desire or intention to tell her.

Her shopping finished, she considered the matter while sipping espresso in Café Pushkin. Pedestrians streamed by outside and weak spring sunshine filtered through the long elegant windows. The driver, who had told her after some urging that his name was Ivan, was waiting outside the door, his arms folded, a veritable bodyguard.

So, Hannah asked herself, was what she didn't know about Sergei going to keep her from attempting this? This relationship that they were meant to have, yet didn't quite seem to be working? Was she going to give it a chance?

Hannah's expression shadowed as she watched a couple stroll by the café, their arms around each other. The woman's face was tilted up towards the man's, the sunshine bathing it in light, yet she already radiated an easy joy from within. Would she and Sergei ever have that? Hannah wondered. Would they ever have anything besides this intense physical attraction, something real and warm and alive?

There had been moments when she'd felt it, felt a pull between them that was not just physical. And Sergei felt it too…

I'm different when I'm with you.

Yet was wanting something enough? After the awkwardness of the last two days and the tension of this morning, Hannah had no answer. Yet she also knew she couldn't walk away. Not yet. So much of her life felt like a lost cause: her abandoned college career, her parents' shop, the awful mess of her relationship with Matthew. She didn't want this to be a lost cause.

She wanted Sergei. She *chose* him, of her own will and strength. And she was willing to fight for him.

An hour later Ivan dropped her off at Sergei's office, despite his misgivings to do so.

'Mr Kholodov said to take you home,' he'd said flatly, and Hannah had smiled sweetly.

'I want to surprise him.'

Ivan had looked as if he didn't think that was a very good idea, but to Hannah's relief he'd agreed to leave her at the office and take her shopping back to the apartment.

Hannah signed in at the sleek front lobby and then rode the lift twenty floors to Kholodov Enterprises.

Grigori was waiting for her by the lift doors. 'Miss Pearl' he said with a nod of his head.

Hannah smiled, genuinely glad to see a familia

remember me,' she said, and Grigori bobbed his head in ac-knowledgement.

'Of course. But I'm afraid Mr Kholodov—'

'Isn't expecting me, I know,' Hannah finished with a wry smile. 'I thought I'd surprise him.'

Grigori frowned, and Hannah's confidence slipped an-other notch. She'd wanted to come here because the thought of waiting back at the apartment for Sergei with her shopping bags all around her felt too passive. Too much like a mistress. If they were going to attempt a *proper* relationship, then she should be able to come to his office without clearing it with him first. She smiled encouragingly at Grigori. 'Is he here?'

'He's in a meeting, but he should be done in a few min-utes,' Grigori said, still sounding reluctant. 'You can wait in the reception area.'

Hannah followed Grigori to an elegant and sleekly modern reception area in front of a pair of formidable wood-panelled doors that Hannah suspected led right to Sergei's office. She sat down in a deep chair that looked a little bit like a banana peel while Grigori went behind his desk and started putting his pile of files away.

She kept her smile and confidence in place for a few min-utes, but as Grigori kept shooting her rather worried glances all the doubts she'd managed to banish earlier came creeping back.

'Tell me, Grigori,' she said, leaning forward, 'how did you come to know Sergei?'

Grigori froze, then swivelled slowly to face her. 'Did he not   you?' he asked, warily, and Hannah smiled and shook

              didn't.'

              rigori filed another folder. 'We grew up together,'
              d, sounding reluctant to part with any infor-

'In the same town?'

Now he looked genuinely startled. 'In the same orphanage.'

'Orphanage—' Hannah stopped, frowning. 'I thought Sergei was raised by his grandmother.'

'He was, until he was eight.'

'And then she died?'

Grigori shook his head. The poor man looked really quite unhappy now, but Hannah wanted to know. Needed to know. 'No, she left Sergei and—' He stopped, corrected himself. 'She left him at the orphanage. She'd had enough.'

Hannah could only stare at him, deeply shocked by such information. How could a woman be so callous towards her own grandchild?

'And what of his parents?'

Grigori shrugged. 'They were never part of his life.' He sighed, shaking his head. 'I shouldn't have told you all this. I'm sure you appreciate, Miss Pearl, what a private man Mr Kholodov is.'

'Yes,' Hannah murmured, 'I do.'

'Please—please don't mention what I told you to Sergei,' Grigori continued. 'I would hate for him to be disappointed in me.' It seemed a strange thing for him to say; disappointed rather than angry. Yet Hannah realised Grigori always spoke of Sergei with a deep respect.

'Of course I won't,' she said, and the ensuing silence was punctuated within seconds by the sound of the panelled doors behind her being opened.

Sergei stood there, his expression focused and yet distant as he spoke to Grigori in staccato Russian. He broke off mid-sentence as he caught sight of Hannah, and for a second, no more, she thought she saw his expression lighten, the beginnings of a smile quirking that wonderfully mo'

Then his features settled into a far more familiar frown and he came towards her.

'What are you doing here?'

'Hello to you too.' It was a little bit of a struggle to rise from the peel-shaped chair, or at least do so elegantly, but somehow Hannah clambered to her feet. Sergei's mouth quirked a tiny fraction and daringly, deliberately, Hannah stood on her tiptoes and kissed him on the mouth. His lips were cool and he did not kiss her back. She tried giving him a playful smile. 'I wanted to surprise you.'

'Surprise me,' Sergei repeated in a tone that suggested he had no idea why she would ever conceive of such a thing.

'Yes, you know, it's *fun.*' She rolled her eyes, trying to keep it all playful even though it took an effort. 'You know that word?' she dared to ask and, after a long, tense moment when Sergei stared at her with absolutely no expression at all, he gave her the faintest glimmer of a smile.

'I don't think I do. But perhaps you could show me.'

Nearly giddy with relief, Hannah grinned, and Sergei smiled back, taking her by the arm. 'Grigori,' he called over his shoulder, 'I'll take the rest of the afternoon off.'

Sergei felt tension coil through him as he took Hannah from his office. Seeing her there had thrown him, both because it had been unexpected and pleasing. He wasn't used to such an emotion, a lightening in his heart. It made him feel uneasy. It had taken effort to smile, to say the right thing. At least, he thought he'd said the right thing, judging by her smile.

She slipped her arm through his as they walked down to the underground garage. A valet had Sergei's private car ready and as Hannah slid inside she gave him a teasing look.

'Do you really need a bullet-proof car to drive around

'Yes.' Sergei slid into the driver's seat and clicked his seat belt.

Hannah, he saw from the corner of his eye, looked a bit taken aback. 'Why?'

He wasn't about to tell her all the reasons why, the kind of people he'd known. His past was his own. 'I am a wealthy man, Hannah. Wealthy men have enemies. And Moscow is not Paris or London.' He gave her a half-smile. 'Having been pickpocketed here, you surely realise that.'

'You can be pickpocketed anywhere.'

'True enough.' He drove out of the garage, flexing his fingers on the steering wheel, wishing he didn't feel so tense. Why couldn't he just enjoy being with Hannah, the way the sunlight glinted off her hair, the sweep of her lashes against her cheek, that teasing smile she'd just given him? Ever since they'd had that wretched conversation things had been difficult. Awkward. And he didn't like it. 'Where do you want to go?' he asked, his voice a little too brusque.

He saw Hannah lift her chin a notch, still determined to be cheerful. An optimist at heart, no matter how cynical she thought she'd become. 'I never did see St Basil's.'

'All right, then.'

Half an hour later they were strolling through the famous cathedral, now a state museum, and Sergei felt himself start to relax. He could do this. If they were just going to stare at some statues, he could definitely do this. And he liked the way Hannah smiled at him, the sound of her laughter, the way her hair brushed his shoulder. Just being with her was enough. It could be.

'Tell me about your childhood,' she said.

What? Every muscle in Sergei's body tightened into a hard knot. 'Why do you want to know?'

Hannah shrugged, her gaze sliding away from his. 'I want to know about you.'

Sergei knew he could be overly suspicious, but he felt bone-deep that something wasn't right here. Hannah wasn't looking at him, and her question had been studiously casual. He stopped, turned her to face him. 'Did Grigori talk to you?'

'Why do you think that?'

'Because you're a terrible liar. What did he tell you?'

She bit her lip. 'He regretted telling me anything. He—he doesn't want you to be disappointed in him.'

'I'm not,' Sergei said flatly. He'd speak to Grigori later. 'What did he tell you?'

'He said the two of you were raised in an orphanage.'

'That's all?'

'Yes—'

Sergei relaxed a fraction. 'Well, it's true enough.'

Her eyes were huge, like violet bruises in her face. 'What was it like?'

He let out a short, sharp laugh, knowing the sound was unpleasant. 'What do you think?'

'Oh, Sergei—'

'Look, there were some kind people. They did their best.' He started walking, quickly, because he didn't want to talk about this.

'How long were you there?' she asked quietly.

'Eight years.'

'*Eight*—'

'I left when I was sixteen.' And he *really* didn't want to talk about that.

She hurried to catch up with him, and as they left the cathedral for the spring sunshine bathing Red Square Sergei felt a deep relief that the subject, for the moment, had been dropped.

She started again that night. They'd had dinner at one of Moscow's best restaurants, and the conversation over their meal had been light, easy, *fun*. Sergei had enjoyed himself, felt himself relax once more. Then as soon as they'd gone back to his penthouse and he'd turned to take her in his arms she'd started again.

'What happened after you left the orphanage?'

Sergei swore under his breath and stalked towards the drinks table where he poured himself a double Scotch. 'Do we really need to talk about this?'

'I want to understand you—'

'And maybe I don't want to be understood.'

He turned back to Hannah, Scotch in hand, and saw how *hurt* she looked. Her face had crumpled as if she was trying not to cry and her eyes were as dark as rain clouds. 'I thought,' she said quietly, 'we were meant to be having a proper relationship.'

Sergei took a deep swallow of Scotch. He intensely regretted ever using those words. What the hell had he been thinking? The problem was, he acknowledged darkly, he *hadn't* been thinking. Not the way he usually did. 'That doesn't mean we have to relive every trivial thing that happened during our childhoods.'

'Not relive it,' Hannah corrected, her voice steady and low. 'But how can we know if anything between us is going to work if we're not honest with one another?'

'Honesty is overrated.'

'Sergei, obviously such a traumatic childhood affected—'

Sergei slammed his glass down on the table, amber liquid sloshing out. 'Don't,' he growled. 'Just don't.'

'Don't what?'

'Don't pity me. Pity is the same as violence, just hidden.'

'I don't pity you. I'm *proud* of you—'

'That's worse.'

'Why? Sergei, whatever happened in your childhood, you've obviously come a long way—'

'Stop it, Hannah.' He turned away, unable to bear the compassion in her violet eyes. It made him feel fourteen years old again, regarded with such quizzical sorrow by the therapists, the couples who wanted to adopt, the people who looked at him as if he were a monkey in a cage. He couldn't bear it from Hannah. 'Stop it,' he said again, quietly. Firmly. 'There is a reason I don't talk about that time of my life. It was a long time ago, and I've put it behind me—'

'Have you?' she inserted quietly, and Sergei's hands clenched into fists.

'You're my lover, not my therapist,' he snapped. 'Stop trying to analyse me.'

'I just want to—'

'Help?' He shook his head. 'Trust me, I've had plenty of people who wanted to help over the years. I prefer the people who don't want to help, who treat you like a human being rather than a charity case. And if you're going to do the same, Hannah, and try to figure me out and feel sorry for me, then we can end it right here.' His voice shook with emotion; his body shook too, and he saw from the widening of Hannah's eyes that she noticed. To hell with it. He was not going to play patient to her do-gooding psychologist, not for one second. 'Right now,' he warned in a low, savage voice, 'I am not interested in *that* kind of relationship.'

She stared at him for a long moment, her expression dark and troubled. Sergei stared back, waiting. It could be her call, if she wanted it to be. But he'd show her the door in the next thirty seconds if she asked him one more damned question about his childhood.

'I'm sorry,' she finally said, quietly. 'You're right. If you don't want to talk about it, I'll respect that.'

Relief flooded through him, relief that was raw and powerful in its intensity, because even though he would have kicked her out right then he had deeply, desperately not wanted to do it.

He crossed the room in two quick strides and pulled her into his arms, kissing her because he needed the contact, even the closeness, and as her arms wrapped around him he knew she did too.

And finally there were no more questions.

CHAPTER ELEVEN

'HERE we are.'

Two hours south of Moscow Sergei turned the car off a country lane onto a private drive lined with birches and lime trees, the arched boughs above sending dappled sunlight onto the avenue below.

'It's beautiful,' Hannah murmured, and Sergei smiled, seeming to relax a fraction. He'd been so tense for most of the ride, even though they'd chatted about nothing more taxing than the weather. Hannah knew she shouldn't have pushed last night, shouldn't have demanded a kind of emotional honesty Sergei wasn't ready to give. He was right too, she knew. She'd been acting as if she meant to fix him, and she knew that wasn't what she really wanted.

She'd spent most of the night lying next to him, trying to figure out just what it was she *did* want, and as dawn sent pale pink fingers of light across the sky she'd finally realised. She wanted to love him…if he'd let her. She didn't let herself think beyond that, or what it might mean for both of them. The realisation, for the moment, was enough.

The car came around a bend and over a little stone bridge that spanned a gentle stream, and there in front of them stood a stately nineteenth-century country house, with two banks of diamond-paned windows and a tower at either end, the reddish stone gleaming in the spring sunlight.

'It's beautiful,' Hannah said as Sergei parked the car and they both got out. The day was warm and drowsy, and a few lazy bumblebees tumbled through the air, a light breeze ruffling the long grass and wildflowers in front of the house. 'So,' she said with a smile, 'this is your home.'

'No.' Sergei shot her a quick answering smile. 'This is my country house. I entertain here.' She shook her head, not understanding, and he beckoned her forward. 'My *home* is a little walk away.'

Sergei easily took both their cases as they walked around the house, the only sound the twitter of birds and the rustle of the wind in the trees. After the frantic pace of both Moscow and Paris, it felt incredibly peaceful. They walked past the landscaped gardens, through an orchard of cherry trees with their tight clusters of little white flowers, past a copse of birches, and then, suddenly, amazingly, they came to a little house.

It was like a fairy house, tiny and enchanted. A little tower poked up one end, and a steep slate roof slanted down the other side, nearly to the ground. A stable door with mullioned glass marked the entrance, and Sergei took a key out of his pocket and unlocked it before beckoning her in.

'My *dacha*.'

Inside the house was all masculine. A little sitting room had walls of bookshelves and several comfortable leather armchairs, with a woodstove in one corner. The kitchen was tucked into a corner on the other side, with a brick floor and an old-fashioned hearth. Upstairs Sergei showed her a rather luxurious-looking bath—the little house was clearly not without its comforts—and the tower housed a single bedroom with a huge king-size bed and not much else.

It was perfect. Hannah turned to Sergei with a big smile. 'I love it.'

Someone from his staff had clearly already been there,

getting things ready, for the kitchen was stocked with a variety of food items from milk and bread to champagne and truffles.

'All the essentials,' Sergei said with a grin as he packed a big woven basket with a sampling of delectable treats, loped a blanket over one arm, and with Hannah in tow headed back out into the sunshine.

They picnicked in a meadow dotted with wildflowers that ran right down to the glassy surface of a small lake. Above them the sky was a deep and abiding blue, the sun lemon-yellow. The day had turned almost hot, so Hannah slipped off her sweater and, leaning back on her elbows, let the warmth wash over her.

Sergei kept handing her things, a perfect little quiche, a strawberry dipped in chocolate, a tumbler of champagne, until finally Hannah clutched her stomach theatrically and shook her head laughing. 'I can't eat another bite, it's all been delicious—'

He leaned over and swiped a drip of chocolate from the corner of her mouth with his thumb. 'I can tell,' he said, and Hannah revelled in seeing him look so relaxed, so at ease. He leaned back on his elbow, his head thrown back, the line of his jaw and throat stark against the sky. He looked beautiful, Hannah thought, with a thud of desire.

'Do you miss the shop?'

Startled, she considered the matter. 'I haven't thought of it once,' she said, 'which I suppose says something.'

Sergei slid her a sideways glance; his eyes looked very blue. 'What does it say?'

She let out a small laugh, although this time the sound held little humour. 'That it's a lost cause, like everything else in my life has been.'

He rolled over to face her, touching her cheek, his touch light as a whisper. *'Everything?'*

'Not everything,' she conceded then sighed, shaking her head. 'I know it sounds terribly self-pitying, and it's not really true. It's just the way it feels sometimes.' She picked a pink daisy that had been waving gently in the breeze and began to pluck its petals. 'I suppose that's why I've been so reluctant to give it up. I didn't want to feel like a failure.'

'By the sounds of it, it wouldn't have been your failure. The shop wasn't doing well long before you took it over.'

'I know that, but in a way that makes me feel worse. Angry anyway. My parents always hid from me how in trouble they were financially. I'd expect that as a child, but as an adult, when I was meant to take the thing over, and all I found were bills and debts—' She let out a weary sigh. 'Anyway, it's not just the shop. I never finished college, and I doubt I ever will. If I sell the shop, if I'm even *able* to sell it, I have no idea what I'll do. And—' She paused, not sure if she could go on, but also knowing that if she ever wanted Sergei to be honest, then she needed to be as well. 'And so far my one attempt at a relationship—a proper one,' she clarified wryly, 'was an unqualified disaster.'

'I hope,' Sergei said mildly, 'you're not talking about us.'

'No. Matthew.' She took a deep breath and let it out slowly. 'You probably don't want to hear about him…' She paused, glancing at him, and although his jaw was tight he smiled wryly.

'Not really. But go on.'

'He came into the shop one day a few weeks after—after my trip. He wasn't from Hadley Springs—he was just passing through on business. He said he was from Albany, but I'm not even sure if that's true. Anyway, he was very charming, very smooth. Too smooth probably, but he seemed so interested in everything—in me—and I fell for it. I wanted to fall.' She swallowed, because she'd wanted what she'd experienced that one magical night with Sergei, and of course she hadn't found it. Sergei had rolled to a sitting position, his elbows braced on his knees.

'Go on,' he said, after a moment, and Hannah had the feeling he knew what she wasn't saying.

'It lasted a few months. He never really told me anything about himself, and he never wanted to go out—just stay in the shop and…well…' She sighed. 'I was still naive then, I suppose, but I bought into it all, never even thinking about how unhappy I was, and then one day a woman came into the shop…' She trailed off, the daisy shredded between her fingers, and Sergei finished softly, 'And it was his wife.'

She let out a shaky laugh. 'Pretty obvious, isn't it? I, of course, was utterly shocked. I confronted him the next time he came in, and he said some terrible things. About me. And why he was with me. And what—what had been between us.' She shook her head, remembering the spite in Matthew's voice, the scorn on his face. She'd felt so low, so *nothing*, and the realisation that she'd given herself to this man shamed her utterly. Even now the memory stung, wounded. 'Anyway, I suppose that's when I stopped believing the best in people. I'd already found my parents' records, how my mother had had me withdrawn from college, the bills and debts, and it—everything—felt like lies.'

Sergei was quiet for a long moment. 'And I had something to do with that, I suppose.'

She couldn't deny it. 'I was hurt by that night,' she said quietly, not quite looking at him. 'You said a lot of hurtful things.'

'I know.'

'Why?' The word was no more than a whisper.

'Because…' Sergei was silent for a long moment. 'I suppose because I was afraid of this.'

'This?'

'This. Us. I'm still afraid.' He gazed at her steadily, his

eyes so very clear, and in their azure depths she could see how honest he was being, and how troubled he was. 'I'm sorry,' he added, his tone low and heartfelt. 'If that helps.'

'It does.'

'But it didn't then,' Sergei acknowledged, and she sighed softly.

'No…at that moment the world was a very bleak place.'

'And now?' Sergei asked softly.

Hannah stared at him, the blue of his eyes, the faint smile curving his lips, the way the sunlight burnished his skin. 'I want to believe again,' she said quietly. 'Like you do.'

'Maybe it's easier than we think,' Sergei murmured. 'Maybe we don't have to be afraid.' He raised his hands and Hannah saw he'd woven together a daisy chain, amazingly delicate, which he placed on her hair like a crown.

'How did you learn to do such a thing,' she exclaimed, reaching up to touch the fragile flowers.

'I've had a lot of practice, although not with daisies. Snowdrops.'

'Really?' She shot him a slightly sceptical look. 'Somehow I didn't think the women you've been with ran to daisy chains for adornment.'

Sergei let out a little laugh, although Hannah thought his eyes looked sad. 'No, they didn't,' he agreed. 'I didn't make chains of flowers for them. I made them for my sister.'

Sister. When had he last spoken that word? Thought it? He had never let himself, yet somehow now with the sunlight pouring over them he'd wanted to say it. He'd wanted to say it to Hannah. Perhaps it was because she'd pushed him with questions last night, or perhaps because she'd stopped when he asked. Perhaps it was because she had been honest now, or maybe honesty was just an instinctive and elemental part of learning to love. Whatever it was, he acknowledged now, to his own amazement, that he wanted to tell her. He wanted to be open with his secrets, just as she had been with hers. Even if it hurt. Especially if it did.

'Snowdrops grew in a corner of the orphanage's yard. Scraggly little things, the only flowers. But Alyona loved them. I told her it was a sign spring was coming, and she never forgot that.'

Hannah adjusted her flower crown, her expression turning serious. 'Alyona,' she said slowly. 'Your sister?'

'Yes. She was—is—ten years younger than me. She came to the orphanage when she was just a baby, and she was adopted when she was four.'

Hannah's eyes widened, shadowed. 'And what about you?'

Amazing that it hurt, even now. Twenty-two years later. 'I was too old.'

'Too *old*? But surely they wouldn't separate siblings?'

He shrugged. 'It's not common practice, no, but this was back when international adoptions were just starting, and things were considerably more lax. I was in a separate facility from Alyona at that point because of our age differences. It was easy for me to be overlooked.'

'You sound very forgiving.'

Did he? How odd, considering the rage and fear and guilt he'd felt and even nurtured for so long. Sergei shook his head. 'No, losing my sister has haunted me for a long time.'

'Overlooked,' Hannah repeated slowly. 'Do you mean the adoptive couple didn't know about you?'

'No, they knew.' Sergei swallowed, tasted bile. He'd never spoken of this to anyone, not even Grigori or Varya. 'They had a therapist come and evaluate me. I didn't pass.'

'*Pass?*'

'I was too damaged, apparently. So the director said. I'm sure he was quite annoyed that he didn't get rid of me when he had the chance.' Tears filled Hannah's eyes, and they almost undid him. He couldn't bear it if she cried, not for him. 'As a surly fourteen-year-old boy, I wasn't exactly an appealing proposition. And at least they saved one person.' He swallowed, remembering Alyona's pale face, the way she'd lifted her chin when she wanted to be brave. He'd never been able to say goodbye. 'It was a long time ago, anyway.'

'I wish I could go back there,' Hannah said with sudden fierceness, 'and punch that stupid director right in the nose.'

Sergei laughed; he couldn't help it. Hannah's reaction was so unexpected, so honest, and completely without pity. 'I've imagined doing the same several times,' he told her dryly. 'Much good it would do me. In any case, orphanages are run much better now, and the laws are better as well. The one I grew up in is actually near here. I've made sure it's much more comfortable than it was, and I visit it personally every time I'm in the area.'

Hannah laid her hand against his cheek. 'You *are* a better man, Sergei,' she whispered. 'A good man. A great one.'

He closed his eyes, tried to swallow past the sudden lump in his throat. He wanted to believe Hannah, but he knew how shocked and horrified she'd be if he told her the rest of his history. His life on the street. His time in prison. Growing up in an orphanage was only the beginning of the sordid story, and he wasn't ready now to tell it to its end.

Trying to smile, he opened his eyes. 'I'm glad you think so,' he said, and kissed her. The kiss was sweet and soft, a fragile promise. Sergei slipped his hands under the heavy mass of Hannah's hair and pulled her to him. She came unresistingly, not only with her body but with her heart. He felt her complete acceptance of him, more powerful than any sensual surrender. He deepened the kiss as she pulled him closer, his hands sliding under her shirt, spanning her ribcage, cupping her breasts.

They lay back down on the grass, moving slowly, sensuously, reveling in this new and deeper intimacy. Clothes snagged, grass scratched, but it couldn't have been more perfect as they moved together, as one, and the sun shone down on them.

It was late afternoon by the time they made it back to the cottage, shaking the grass from their clothes and trailing blankets and daisy chains.

'We need a bath,' Sergei announced, and Hannah gave him an impish smile.

'I did notice that tub was big enough for two.'

'And,' Sergei agreed solemnly, 'we don't want to waste any water.'

The tub was indeed big enough for two, and plenty of hot water and bubbles besides. Sergei didn't think he'd ever experienced anything as sweetly erotic as Hannah nestled against him, her hair and body wet and gleaming, as she took a flannel and began to slowly soap his chest.

'How,' she asked slowly, 'did you go from orphan to millionaire? You must be incredibly smart.'

He gave a little laugh. 'Lucky, more like.' He'd been in the right place at the right time more than once.

She glanced up at him, her eyes dark and serious. 'Luck only takes you so far. You have to have talent and determination too. And sometimes that doesn't even see you through.' He knew she was thinking of her little shop, but then her expression cleared and she gave him a playful smile. 'I don't even know what this Kholodov Enterprises of yours does.'

'Nothing illegal, if that's what you're worried about.' She was driving him slightly crazy with the slow, mesmerising way she was drawing lazy circles on his body, popping any bubbles with a gentle, exploratory finger.

'I wasn't thinking that!' she protested, and Sergei hauled her up so her legs were wrapped around his waist, her body pressed intimately against his.

'Now this,' he said with a wicked little smile, 'is getting interesting.'

He shifted, deliberately, and Hannah gasped aloud. *'Oh—'*

Sergei slipped his hands around her bottom and drew her even closer. 'Now what were you saying?' he asked, eyebrows innocently arched.

'Something—about—business—' Hannah managed, her expression glazing, lips parting, and as Sergei finally sank inside her both of them stopped speaking altogether.

Later, dressed only in Sergei's dressing gown with the sleeves rolled up past her elbows and her hair piled on top of her head, Hannah made them both eggs and toast.

'It's not much, I know, but I'm afraid I'm not much of a cook.'

'Good thing I like eggs.'

They ate in front of the wood stove, balancing their plates on their laps, and Sergei didn't think he'd ever seen anything as unbearably sweet as Hannah in his dressing gown, a forkful of egg held aloft.

'So what does Kholodov Enterprises *do*, exactly?'

More questions. He didn't mind them as much now, but they still made him feel uncomfortable. Tense. There were still things he hadn't told Hannah, terrible things, shocking things. Things he was afraid would horrify her, and make her change her mind. 'A bit of everything. Mainly property and technology, but I'm willing to take on whatever looks profitable.'

She gazed at him seriously. 'And what do you like most about it?'

Sergei considered the question. 'The feeling of accomplishment, I suppose,' he said, 'and stability.'

'And do you ever keep in touch with anyone from the...' She stopped slowly, realisation dawning. 'Grigori.'

'Yes.'

'And Ivan too, probably.' Sergei nodded. Hannah didn't speak for a moment, still thinking. 'And Varya,' she finally said, softly, and Sergei just shrugged.

Hannah leaned forward, touching his cheek, her fingers as light as a whisper. 'Was there anyone you didn't try to save?' she asked, and he let out a laugh that sounded far too harsh in the fire-lit intimacy of the room.

'Plenty of people. And plenty of people don't even want to be saved.'

She nodded slowly. 'Yes, I've come to realise you can't make someone want something, can you?'

Sergei was kept from answering by the buzz of his mobile phone. He hesitated, then, with a quick, apologetic glance at Hannah, reached for it. 'It could be important,' he murmured, and felt his heart freeze when he saw who the call was from. The private investigator he'd hired.

'Yes?'

'Mr Kholodov? I have news.'

Sergei angled his body slightly away from Hannah. 'And?' he asked, his voice terse.

'I've found her, Mr Kholodov. I've found Alyona.'

CHAPTER TWELVE

SERGEI's fingers clenched around the phone. He was conscious of his own hard-thudding heart, of Hannah hearing every word, and of the gnawing fear inside him that made him wonder if he even wanted to hear any more.

'Tell me,' he finally said, his voice low, and then listened as the investigator recited his newly found facts.

'She goes by the name of Allison Whitelaw. She lives in San Francisco. She's twenty-six years old—'

'I know *that*—'

'Works as a nursery school teacher. Unmarried. I have her phone number and email address.'

Sergei swallowed. He felt dizzy, his mouth so dry he had to force the words out. 'Give them to me, please.'

'Would you like me to make contact first?' the investigator asked, his tone carefully tactful. 'Sudden contact can be—distressing—for some. Sometimes having an intermediary helps.'

'I see.' Sergei could feel Hannah's curiosity like a palpable thing. He turned away a little more. 'Yes, perhaps you should—initiate contact first. I'll send you the draft of an email today.'

'Very good.'

'I'd like you to—to contact her as soon as possible.'

'Understood.'

Sergei disconnected the call and then turned back to Hannah. She bent to clear their plates, her hair falling from its clip, a tendril resting against her cheek. 'That was delicious, if I do say so myself,' she murmured, taking the plates to the little kitchen, and with a pang of something between regret and relief Sergei realised she wasn't going to ask any questions.

He watched her for a moment, rinsing and stacking the plates in the sink, positively swimming in his dressing gown, and he realised with a sudden fierceness how good she looked standing there, in his home, the only home he'd ever felt he'd had. And not just good, but *right,* right in a bone-deep way that made him blurt, 'That call—it was from a private investigator. He's been looking for Alyona.'

She turned slowly. 'And did he find her?'

'Yes.'

'Oh, Sergei—'

'He's been looking, on and off, for over a year,' Sergei said quietly. 'Since I met you.' Hannah shook her head, not understanding, and he continued, 'I'd never tried to look for her before because I didn't want to think about it. About her. I wanted to forget, and I was also afraid of what I might find if I did look for her. Maybe she'd forgotten me.' Hannah said nothing, although he saw the sorrow reflected in the storm of her eyes. 'Then I met you, and you amazed me with your innocence and optimism, even if I seemed like I scorned it.' He gave her a small smile. 'And I decided to look. And then I— What is the expression? I chickened out and stopped. And then started again. And now she's been found, living in California.' He shook his head slowly, still trying to process the news.

'After so many years,' Hannah said softly. 'It must be hard to imagine.'

'It is.'

'Are you going to contact her?'

'Yes. We'll see.' How would Alyona react? Would she even remember him? Hannah crossed to him suddenly, put her arms around him and drew him into a fierce hug.

'Oh, Sergei,' she said, 'how exciting it is.'

And as he put his arms around her and drew her close, he believed her.

They had three days. Three days of lazing and lounging around, of long, meandering walks and a few swims and lots of making love. They were a wonderful three days, and even though Hannah could tell Sergei was anxious about contacting Alyona, he didn't let it detract from their time together, and that both humbled and gratified her.

He was, she realised, quite an incredible man, and she was completely in love with him. It had been easy after all. Amazingly easy, so it was hard to believe that only a few days ago she'd been sitting morosely in a Moscow café wondering if any of it would work.

It was working wonderfully now, and it did for those three days. Then everything began to come crashing down.

It started with a phone call. Sergei's mobile phone buzzed while they were out on a walk through the estate, following twisting paths through a cluster of pines, the air cool and damp. He reached for it, and Hannah tensed as she saw his face cloud, his brows snap together.

'What has happened?'

That was all she heard, for the rest of the conversation was conducted in hurried Russian. Yet Hannah understood the urgent, upset tone, and she knew with a sinking certainty that their idyll was over.

Several minutes later Sergei slid his phone back into his pocket. 'We have to return to Moscow.'

'What's happened?'

Sergei hesitated, his mouth hardening. He almost looked angry, and with a tremor of fear Hannah wondered if their relationship could survive reality. Maybe anyone could fall in love in the Russian countryside, with champagne and truffles and bubble baths for two.

'Sergei?' she prompted quietly, and his glance slid away from her.

'It's Varya,' he said, and that was all.

They packed mostly in silence, the little house seeming almost reproachful at their sudden departure. Even the sky had darkened with rain clouds, and as Sergei threw their cases in the back of his car the first drops began to fall.

'What's happened with—with Varya?' Hannah finally ventured to ask as they drove away from the house, the trees lining the avenue bowed down under the wind and rain. Even though she knew nothing had happened between Sergei and Varya—at least she didn't *think* anything had happened— just saying the woman's name reminded her of that painful, humiliating episode, the way Sergei had snugged his arm around Varya's waist and told Hannah to leave, and now her doubts and uncertainties came creeping back.

'She's been hurt,' Sergei said shortly. 'Again.'

'Again?'

His hands tensed and flexed on the steering wheel, his expression like granite. 'Varya is always getting into trouble. I've—I've tried to help her, but she resists.' He lowered his head, his expression unbearably grim. 'Like you said, you can't make someone want something.'

They drove mostly in silence back to Moscow. The rain had stopped, the sky clearing to a fragile, wispy blue as Sergei pulled into the car park of one of Moscow's best hospitals.

Clearly the staff was aware of Sergei's wealth and power, for they fairly snapped to attention as he stalked through the hospital entrance. Grigori was waiting outside Varya's room, his expression so fatigued and desperate that Hannah's heart immediately ached for him.

He spoke quickly in Russian to Sergei, and she saw Sergei grasp Grigori's wrist and clap him on the shoulder in an expression of comfort and sympathy.

Hannah waited, anxious, unneeded, as Sergei spoke to doctors and nurses, and then went alone into Varya's room. It was absolutely absurd to feel jealous, Hannah told herself. She knew that. And she didn't feel jealous, not exactly, just… insecure. Whatever was between her and Sergei was still too new to be tested like this. She was afraid it might not survive.

Grigori took a seat next to her in the waiting room. Although still clearly worried, he gave her a shy smile. 'There is a saying in Russian—"Love is like a mouse falling into a box. There is no way out."'

Hannah managed a smile back. 'That's rather a grim saying.'

'But true, yes?'

'Yes,' she conceded with a sigh, and when Grigori nodded in vigorous yet rather resigned agreement, the penny finally dropped. 'Varya,' she said slowly. 'You love her?'

Grigori spread his hands. 'Since we were children. We stayed together in the orphanage, two gawky dreamers. Sergei always protected us.'

A lump rose in Hannah's throat. 'Did he?' she whispered. She could believe that, picture it even.

'And then also when we left the orphanage—Sergei is a year older than us. He left first, and then he came and fetched us when Varya and I turned sixteen.' He shook his head. 'It is a fearsome thing—to be out on the street with nothing but the clothes on your back, but that's how it was in those days. Sergei made sure we had food, a place to stay, but Varya…' He sighed. 'She caught the attention of a boy. A man, really, he was maybe twenty. The head of a gang.' He shook his head. 'It was not good for her.'

'No, I imagine not,' Hannah said quietly, although in truth she could hardly imagine any of it.

'Sergei tried to protect her, but she wouldn't have it. She has always been proud, Varya. Proud and ashamed all at the same time. And then when Sergei went—' He stopped, shaking his head. 'But I talk too much. Sergei would not like me to say these things.' He gave her a small, hesitant smile. 'You love him.'

Hannah blushed but nodded. 'Yes.'

Grigori nodded back, slowly, considering. 'It is good for him. No one has loved him before. Not like that, the love of a woman.' He smiled, adding, 'There is another saying in Russia. "You cannot live without the sun, and you cannot live without your beloved."' The door to the waiting room opened and Grigori stood. 'I pray it goes well with you,' he said quietly, and turned to Sergei.

Sergei looked unbearably tired and sad, his face haggard and unshaven. 'She wants to see you, Grigori,' he said. 'Perhaps you can make her see sense.'

He turned to Hannah, his expression turning terribly bland, and Hannah felt her heart clench. He was closing himself off. Again. She could see it, sense it, and she didn't know what to do.

'Sergei—'

'It's late. Let's go home.'

Home. That was encouraging, at least. Wordlessly Hannah followed him out of the hospital.

They didn't speak all the way back to the penthouse.

Sergei unlocked the door, and before he'd even flicked on the lights he turned to Hannah, pulling her roughly into his arms and kissing her with a kind of sorrowful desperation that made her heart ache even as desire flooded through her and she kissed him back with every ounce of her love and every fibre of her being.

Then suddenly Sergei thrust her away and stalked to the other side of the room, his back to her, facing the night. Hannah leaned against the door, her legs watery, her body aching. 'Sergei, what's going on?' she asked in as steady a voice as she could manage.

'It's always the same,' he said in a low voice. He drove his fingers through his hair and then wearily dropped them to his sides. 'Nothing ever changes.'

'I can understand,' Hannah said, 'why you feel that way right now—'

'Can you?' Sergei cut her off harshly. 'You have no idea.' He drew in a shuddering breath, his back still to her. 'No idea how it feels, like you can never escape your past, the person you were. Like a ghost it haunts you.' He gave a bitter laugh. 'I am my own ghost. And Varya feels the same. It never lets you go, never leaves you alone.' He shook his head, his body blazing tension. 'And you have no idea what we've seen, what we've *done*—you've been in your cosy little world and you just have no—damned—*clue!*' His voice rang out, loud with anger, ragged with pain.

Hannah took a deep breath, let it out slowly. 'You're right,' she said quietly, 'I don't.'

'I'm sorry,' he said after a moment. 'I shouldn't have shouted at you. I shouldn't have expected you to understand.'

You weren't, Hannah wanted to say. *You were expecting me not to understand, and I want to. Don't close me off, Sergei, please.*

But she didn't get a chance to say any of it, because Sergei's mobile phone buzzed and he reached for it with a resigned air.

Hannah tensed, a sudden, awful premonition rippling through her that this phone call was going to change everything. Change *them*. Her mouth dried, and she tried to speak. 'Sergei, don't—'

'Hello?' Hannah watched, holding her breath, as Sergei listened intently, tension tautening his body even further.

'Thank you,' he said after a minute or two of silence from his end, his voice icily polite. 'Thank you very much.' He disconnected the call, his back still to Hannah.

'What—'

'Excuse me,' he said softly, so softly, and somehow that made it worse. Death came with a whisper.

For as Sergei left the room, closing the bedroom door behind him with a final little click, Hannah had a terrible feeling that something monumental had just happened, in the space of a few seconds. Something terrible.

CHAPTER THIRTEEN

SERGEI stared blindly out of the bedroom window, his heart beating with hard, painful thuds as the private investigator's words echoed relentlessly through him.

She does not wish to have any further contact. I'm sorry.

Alyona didn't want to see him. Didn't want even to email him. No further contact at all. After over twenty years of missing her, a year of searching for her, a *lifetime* of loving her, to be so summarily and utterly rejected was unbearable.

Sergei sank onto the edge of the bed and dropped his head in his hands. No, he realised with sudden, wrenching clarity, what was unbearable was having hoped at all. He hadn't wanted to hope, which was why he hadn't tried to find her until now. Until Hannah.

Hannah, with her shy smile and soft words and violet eyes, with her sweetness and her rosy, *ridiculous* view of the world, *Hannah* had made him hope. Hannah had made him believe— *want* to believe—in happy endings. Happy endings that didn't exist, not for men like him. And the fact that he'd let her do it filled him with an unbearable rage.

He stood up, pacing the room restlessly, each memory— each *face*—rising up to mock him.

His grandmother's snarling face, telling him she hadn't wanted him, his parents hadn't wanted him. Nobody had. He still could see the look of almost bored disinterest on her face as she held his wrist to inflict his 'punishments'—the cigarette burns that lined his right arm.

The indifferent faces of the orphanage workers, or even the faces of the kind ones, who couldn't look at him without their features twisting with pity. The faces of volunteers and therapists who came in and tried to help, and couldn't hide their horror.

The blunt faces of the gangs on the street, who only wanted him if he could steal or sell something. It didn't matter what it was. The anguished face of someone he'd beaten bloody in yet another street battle.

The smug face of the warden when he was finally sent down for robbery, the utter despair on the faces of the prisoners.

So many faces.

And then finally, most painfully, the shock and sorrow on Hannah's face…when he told her he couldn't do this. He couldn't let himself hope any more. He couldn't change.

The realisation was like a hammer blow to his heart, shattering the illusions he'd allowed himself to secretly nurture, and for that he had to be grateful. He couldn't believe he'd let it get this far.

Slowly, with aching determination, Sergei rose from the bed. He knew what he had to do, and it filled him with a deep and angering anguish. He didn't *want* to feel this, to feel so much, but surely it was better to end it now than to continue, knowing there was no future.

Hannah paced the living room, nearly dizzy with nerves, her heart thudding hard. She didn't know who had called Sergei, what had been said, but none of it was good. And she had a terrible, treacherous feeling that when he came out of the bedroom—*if* he did—he was going to tell her it was over. *They* were.

She stopped in front of the window, stared out at the black

night. She felt sorrow and frustration and a sudden, fierce rage all rise up in her because half of her wanted to fight for Sergei, and half of her didn't want to have to. She leaned her forehead against the cold glass and closed her eyes. She was tired of fighting. Tired of being disappointed. Hurt. Rejected.

At some point in your life, Hannah, you'll find out that people disappoint you. Deceive you. I find it's better to accept it and move on than let yourself continually be let down.

Maybe Sergei had been right when he'd told her that a year ago. Maybe she would have been better off if she'd believed him. Instead here she was now, her splintering heart flinging itself against her chest, desperation and sorrow and a jagged little shard of hope all a broken tangle inside her.

Maybe, Hannah thought, tears stinging her eyes, now was the time to walk away.

Except she desperately didn't want to. She wanted to stay because she loved Sergei. Love, Hannah realised, was a choice, a choice she was in control of, a choice she had made deliberately, and she knew what love did. Love stayed. Love believed. Love hoped.

The door opened.

Hannah turned. She saw immediately from the composed and yet determined look on Sergei's face that he wasn't about to sweep her in his arms and kiss her. He did not have good news.

'Who called you?'

Sergei flicked a hand in dismissal. 'It doesn't matter.'

'Yes, it does, because—'

'No,' he cut off in a tone of lethal softness, a tone she hadn't heard in days, no, a *year*. 'It doesn't.'

Hannah swallowed, painfully reminded of the man in Red Square who had looked at her with such disbelieving disdain. 'What's going on, Sergei?' she asked quietly.

'I can't do this, Hannah.' He sounded very cold. 'I thought

I could, I thought I could try a real relationship, but I can't. I'm sorry.' He spoke flatly, without any inflection, any emotion at all, and it made Hannah wonder if this was the same man who had held her in his arms, who had touched her like a treasure, who had wiped the tears from her cheek.

'Why?'

'I just can't.' He looked away.

'And that's it?' She stared at him in both rising disbelief and fury. 'No reasons, no excuses at least?' He hesitated. It wasn't much, but Hannah grabbed on to it. 'You have to at least give me a reason, Sergei. Something to show me *why*—' She broke off, drew in a shuddering, hiccuppy breath.

Slowly he swung his gaze around, his ice-blue eyes freezing her to the floor, his expression utterly unyielding. 'I don't have to give you anything, Hannah. Not even a reason.'

Hannah jerked back at the icy indifference in his tone. It was the voice of a stranger. 'So that's really it, then?'

'Yes.'

She shook her head slowly, words crowding her throat. *But you kissed me so softly. You told me your secrets. You lay in my arms.* She didn't say any of it. Couldn't. It occurred her to then, with a sudden, painful ferocity, that Sergei might have been lying all along. Perhaps he'd never intended to have a *real* relationship. That had just been a ploy to soften her up. Perhaps this was the kind of ending he'd planned, right from the beginning. She swallowed and finally managed to speak. 'So is this how you end it with all your mistresses?'

He stared at her without expression for a good thirty seconds before answering with a shrug, 'More or less. Sometimes I give them a bracelet.' Hannah gasped aloud. She could not believe he could be so cruel. 'However,' Sergei continued flatly, 'since I already gave you that choker...' He shrugged again and turned towards the bedroom. 'Ivan will see you to the airport,' were his last words to her.

The door closed shut with a final click, and Hannah stood there alone, disbelieving, shaking, and then suddenly, amazingly, *hugely* furious. Without even thinking about what she was doing she flew to the door Sergei had just closed. It was, of course, locked. That didn't stop her.

Hannah pounded on the door with her fists, hit it hard enough to hurt her hands. 'Coward!' she shouted. 'You're nothing but a coward, Sergei Kholodov! You're hiding behind that stupid tough guy thing you do because you're scared! The minute this oh-so *real* relationship of ours gets a little tricky, a little less picnics and flowers and great sex, you're pulling the plug and *that*—makes *you*—a *coward*!' The words poured from her, welling up from a place of pain and truth deep inside. The only answer was silence.

Breathless, Hannah sank to the floor and drew her knees up to her chest, all her fury gone, leaving her flatter than ever. She might as well have said nothing. The door remained closed, the room beyond silent.

Hannah lay her cheek against her knees. She wished she could cry, but the pain cut to deep for mere tears. She supposed she should get up, pack, wait for Ivan, yet something in her rebelled against making it too easy for Sergei. She would not tiptoe away with her pay-off choker and a suitcase full of clothes she'd never wanted.

Yet what could she do? Sit here on the floor like a pathetic, kicked puppy yearning for its master's touch?

She heard the click of a lock turning and then the door behind her opened. Hannah scooted away, lurched to her feet. Sergei stood in the doorway, colour blazing on his cheekbones, his eyes glittering like cold sapphires.

'I am not,' he said in a low, clear voice, 'a coward.'

'Then prove it,' Hannah snapped. 'Prove it by not running away the first time things get tough!'

Sergei's features contorted, although whether in anger or

sorrow or something else entirely Hannah could not say. She glared at him, her body as tense as a bow, tightly strung, taking aim. 'Tell me,' she demanded.

'Tell you what?'

'Who telephoned you, for starters.'

He folded his arms, his gaze narrowed, his expression turning indifferent, but Hannah knew better. She knew just how much feeling Sergei could hide. 'It was the private investigator I hired.'

'About Alyona?' Sergei gave the barest of nods, and Hannah knew then what the news must have been. *Damn.* 'Why?' she whispered.

'If you're asking why she is refusing any further contact, I'd say the answer is obvious. She's moved on to better things. She has her own life now, has had it for years, and it doesn't include me.'

'But not even to ask—' Hannah stopped, knowing there was no point, not now. 'So,' she said slowly, 'you suffer one setback and you decide to cut me out of your life?'

'Don't,' Sergei warned her coldly, 'trivialise.'

'Sergei, that's the last thing I want to do.' Hannah spread her hands and saw they were trembling. She didn't care. Let Sergei see how he affected her, how afraid she was. Maybe then he wouldn't hide his own feelings so much. 'The very last thing. If anything, my problems seem trivial compared to what you've endured—'

'Don't pity me, either,' Sergei growled and she dropped her hands.

'I *don't*. But I do pity any child who endured what you did. Don't you?'

Her question seemed to startle him for his eyes widened, his body stilling. He didn't speak for a few moments. 'Yes,' he finally said quietly. 'I do.'

Hannah sagged a little. She felt as if she'd won a victory,

although she couldn't even say what it was. And still the war raged on, around and ahead. So many battles to fight. 'So why did you tell me it won't work between us?' she finally asked, her voice thankfully steady.

Sergei shoved his hand in his pockets and let out a long, weary sigh. 'Because I don't think it will,' he finally said, 'and it's not just Alyona. It's everything. Seeing Varya in that hospital room, knowing she'll never change—'

'You,' Hannah said, 'are not Varya.'

He inclined his head. 'Indeed not, but still.' He looked at her with a grave sorrow. 'I'm more like Varya than you think.'

'What on earth is that supposed to mean?'

'It means,' Sergei told her, his voice gaining an edge, 'that I've seen and done things that would have you running a mile. Things that would fill you with horror and disgust and despair.' He spoke flatly, calmly even, but Hannah saw how the muscles in his jaw had bunched, his shoulders set rigid. 'I'm not the man you think I am.'

'You're not the man you think you are, either,' Hannah said quietly.

'And I thought you weren't an optimist any longer,' Sergei returned, a slight sneer in his voice. Hannah had a sudden vivid memory of standing in that private room, staring at Sergei and telling him what she'd believed deeply in her heart.

You're trying to push me away and I'm not sure why. Maybe it's because you're afraid of hurting me, or maybe you're just afraid. You're a better man than you think you are.

She'd believed it then, and she believed it now. She lifted her chin. 'I'm not an optimist, Sergei. Nor am I naive. Right now I see things very clearly, and I think you're afraid, just as you told me you were before.'

'I am not afraid.'

'Afraid,' Hannah continued, 'that this relationship could work. I'm not saying I'm an expert on relationships, far from it. But I'm willing to risk my heart and give it—us—a chance, and that doesn't just mean romantic little getaways or luxury hotels. It means real life and hard work, up and down. I'm willing to face that. Are you?'

'I *know*,' Sergei told her, 'this relationship won't work.'

'Because you're not capable of it?' Hannah said, scornfully, and Sergei just bunched his jaw. 'You don't think you're capable of loving someone? Is that it?' She heard the contempt in her voice, and Sergei heard it too. She could tell by the narrowing of his eyes and the tightness of his jaw that it made him furious. Well, *good*. 'I might believe that,' she said more quietly, 'if I hadn't seen you in the hospital with Varya. Or even with Grigori. Or heard you talk about Alyona. You're perfectly capable of loving people, Sergei. In fact I think you have a *lot* of love to give. So that's not what's making you push me away.'

'Don't—'

'So,' Hannah continued, her voice growing stronger, surer, 'it must be something else. Maybe it's that you're afraid *I* won't love *you*.'

His eyes flashed dark and his mouth thinned. 'Do you?' he asked, his tone caught between a supplication and a sneer.

'Do I what?' Hannah challenged him softly.

A muscle flickered in his temple. 'Do you love me?' he clarified, his voice no more than a hoarse whisper. But before Hannah could answer—answer with a resounding, heartfelt *yes*—Sergei continued. 'Do you love the man who left the orphanage at sixteen to pickpocket tourists like yourself on the street?'

Her eyes widened. 'So that's how you knew what those kids were doing.'

'And I didn't stop at pickpocketing, Hannah. I was big and strong and so that made me useful. Intimidating.'

'I'll agree with that,' she said, keeping her voice as wry as she could, although her heart had started to thud. Sergei was looking at her with a grim determination, and yet from the veiled look in his eyes she had a feeling he wasn't seeing her at all.

'I joined a gang,' he said flatly. 'A street gang. Thugs. We dealt in whatever sordid vice was profitable—cigarettes, alcohol and…'

'You had to survive,' Hannah said steadily, but Sergei hardly seemed to hear her.

'And because I was so big and strong? You know what I did?' She tensed, tried to keep her face neutral, bland. A single flinch, she feared, would condemn her and Sergei both. 'I provided the muscle,' Sergei clarified, his voice still flat and without emotion, although Hannah could see how tight he held his jaw, his shoulders, his fists clenched at his sides. 'I dealt with anyone who needed a little talking to—with my fists.'

She blinked. Said nothing. She knew Sergei had more to say, and he was saying it as much for his own sake as for hers. She wondered if he'd ever told anyone all this before. It was like a bloodletting, the drainage of a wound. 'I didn't even know their names. Or what they did. I just saw their faces. So many faces.'

Hannah's heart ached. She thought of Grigori's words at the hospital—*Sergei made sure we had food, a place to stay*—and she thought she knew why Sergei had done it all. Not so he could survive, but so that they could.

'And then,' Sergei continued, 'it ended. When I was nineteen I was sent to prison for my part in a robbery. Since I was just the lookout, I only got five years.' He tapped his chest, at the place of his crucifix tattoo. 'Prison tattoo. Shows I was in for robbery. And the spires on my back show the number of years.'

Three spires, Hannah knew. Three years. In *prison*. She

blinked again. 'That,' she said after a moment, 'must have been terrible.'

He let out a short laugh. 'Living hell. The prisons are over-crowded, raging with tuberculosis, and the guards appoint their pet favourites to act as enforcers—you can imagine the kind of abuse of power that leads to.' He shook his head slowly. 'There is no hope in prison.'

'But you got out,' Hannah reminded him, because from the bleak look in Sergei's eyes it almost seemed as if he were still behind those bars.

'Yes. Early, for good behaviour. And in some ways prison was good for me, because it made me determined never to go back to the gangs. The street.'

He would have been twenty-two, Hannah surmised. Without family, home, or any resources at all. 'What did you do?' she whispered.

'I got a job doing menial jobs for an electronics firm. That's what I did in prison—worked on an assembly line for electronics. I learned a lot.'

'And then?'

He shrugged. 'I worked hard. I listened. I studied at night. Business, English, whatever I could. And one day I heard two executives arguing about a glitch in the latest cell phone and I made a suggestion. They took it, and I made sure I got credit.'

'That intimidation thing again.'

He gave her a tiny smile, although his eyes were still hard and cold. 'Something like that.'

Hannah shook her head slowly. 'And within ten years, you owned that company,' she guessed.

'Five.'

'Sergei, you're amazing.' She walked towards him, smiling, stopping when he shook his head violently.

'Didn't you just hear anything I *said*?'

'Yes—'

'I was in a gang. In *prison*. I beat people up, broke somebody's arm—'

'I heard all that.'

'I sold—'

'Are you *trying* to put me off?'

'There are things about me, Hannah, things you don't want to know—'

'Probably,' she agreed steadily. 'And trust me, I don't need a laundry list of every shameful thing you've ever done.' He let out a shuddery breath, as if she'd proved his point. Hannah gazed at him, steady, unyielding. 'Do you do those things now?'

He jerked back. 'No, of course not.'

'You told me Kholodov Enterprises is legit,' Hannah reminded him. 'Is it?'

His eyes flashed anger. *'Yes.'*

'And you don't go around breaking people's arms…do you?'

He glared at her, let out a huff of breath. 'No.'

She nodded slowly. 'So I'm supposed to recoil in disgust and say I can't love you because you did terrible things when you were young and frightened?'

Now he looked really angry. 'Now you know what I'm capable of.'

'Yes. I know you're capable of rising from the gutter of life to stand on the top. I know you're capable of working hard when everyone and everything is against you so you can succeed, and not just for yourself, but for those you love. Where were Grigori and Varya during all this time?'

Startled, he narrowed his eyes. 'Doing the best they could.'

'I bet Grigori made a good thief,' Hannah mused. 'No one would suspect him. He looks so trustworthy.'

'Grigori never stole anything,' Sergei hissed, all offended anger that she could suggest such a thing.

'Oh, I *see*. Only you did. And then you gave them food and money and made sure they never had to do the dirty work.'

'*Don't* blame them—'

'Then stop blaming yourself,' Hannah snapped, and she sounded almost as angry as he did. 'Stop beating yourself up for what you did all those years ago. You *survived*, Sergei. You succeeded, and you took as many people with you as you could, even the ones who didn't want to come. Where would Varya be without you? Or Grigori? Or Ivan? Or any of the others?' She closed the space between them, stared up at him with all the openness and honesty and love that she could. 'I'm proud of you, and I don't mean that in a patronising, pitying way. I'm *humbled* by what you accomplished, the strength of spirit you had, and that you came through it all to be the man you are now. A better man than I even knew.'

She reached up on her tiptoes to cradle his face, her thumbs brushing his lips. 'I love you, Sergei. I love the man you are now, and that includes the man and even the boy you were, and how you became who you are now. I think you're amazing and strong and really rather wonderful.' Her voice choked and she blinked back tears. Tried to smile. 'And if you kissed me now, I'd be really, really happy.'

The moment stretched on as Sergei stared at her, a look of almost scornful incredulity on his face, and Hannah stood there, waiting, wondering. Had she just bared her soul to be rejected again, and this time worse than ever? Then his expression slowly changed to something far sweeter. Gratitude. Joy. *Hope.*

He smiled, a thing of tremulous wonder, and then his arms came around her and his lips were on hers, seeking, demanding and treasuring all at once, every memory and hope and dream wrapped up in that one wonderful kiss. And Hannah was happy.

Really happy.

CHAPTER FOURTEEN

HANNAH woke up slowly, stretching, savouring the sunshine that streamed through Sergei's bedroom windows, his arm comfortably heavy across her middle. She curled into him, wrapping her arms around his waist, feeling as smugly contented as a cat. After the emotional exhaustion of the last twenty-four hours, last night had ended really rather wonderfully. And even though she did not yet know what the future held—after Sergei had shared all the secrets of his past they hadn't done much more talking—she felt hopeful. Really hopeful, deep down, with an unshakeable certainty that wasn't based on youthful naiveté or innocent optimism but on experience. On faith. On love.

Sergei stirred and pulled her closer. Hannah rested her cheek against his shoulder, breathing in the scent of him. His hand found her own still wrapped around his waist and his fingers threaded with hers. Neither of them spoke; Hannah's heart was too full. She had a feeling Sergei's might be as well.

'We need to go back to the hospital,' he said after a moment, and Hannah's heart skipped a beat at the *we*. They were in this—in everything—together. 'To see Varya.'

'Okay.'

He squeezed her fingers. 'I've tried everything with her,' he said quietly. 'Offered her money, a place to live, a job, doctors and therapists. She won't take any of it, only a little cash when she's truly desperate.' He sighed, his fingers still threaded with hers. 'What can I do?' he asked, the question so simple, so heartfelt.

'Maybe you're not the one who needs to do something now,' Hannah said after a moment. 'Maybe someone else needs to step up.'

'Who?'

'Can't you think of one person?'

He shifted so he could look at her. 'You mean Grigori?'

'He loves her.'

'I know.'

She smiled and curved her body closer to his. 'Somehow I thought you might say that.'

Sergei shook his head, his expression shadowed. 'I don't know what good can come of it. As far as I know, Varya has never looked at Grigori like that, and she seems bent on a course to destroy herself.'

Hannah touched his cheek. 'We can still hope.'

'Yes…but is it enough?'

His question seemed to hang in the air between them, breaking the intimacy of the moment. Was Sergei talking about Varya and Grigori, Hannah wondered, or about themselves? After everything that had happened last night, did he still doubt?

As he slid from the bed and disappeared into the bathroom Hannah realised he did. Of course he did. One conversation, one night, did not change a lifetime of hurt, uncertainty, pain and guilt. Building this relationship was going to take time. Sighing, she rolled onto her back and closed her eyes against the sunlight still streaming through the window.

An hour later they arrived at the hospital. Grigori met them at the door to Varya's room, looking haggard and unshaven still wearing the same clothes as yesterday.

'How is she?' Sergei asked in a low voice, speaking English for Hannah's sake.

'Better,' Grigori said firmly, and Sergei raised his eyebrows in silent query. 'She realises she needs to change, Serozhya. I—' He glanced shyly at Hannah before continuing, 'I told her I loved her. I never had before.'

A faint smile tugged at Sergei's mouth. 'And?'

Grigori sighed. 'Well, she did not tell me she loved me. I did not expect it. But at least she has agreed to come home with me. I will take care of her there. Make sure she has proper food and medicine, and that she is safe. She is happy for that.' He lifted his shoulder in a half-apologetic shrug. 'It is not much, perhaps, and not as much as I would wish. But it is something.'

Sergei clapped Grigori on the shoulder. 'I am glad to hear it, Grisha,' he said softly.

Grigori led them into Varya's room, and Hannah was amazed by the sight of the woman who had once seemed like a threat to her. Now Varya's face was free of garish make-up, her slender body clad only in a hospital gown. Her blond hair, still the brassy shade from a bottle, was tucked behind her ears. She looked young and vulnerable, Hannah thought, despite the lines apparent on her face. She had to be thirty-five, a year younger than Sergei.

'Serozhya.' She held her hands out to Sergei and he clasped them warmly. She spoke in Russian, and Grigori quietly translated for Hannah.

'She says she is seeing sense at last.' He looked down, battling both pride and embarrassment. 'I have shown her, she says.'

Sergei spoke in Russian and then English. 'I am so glad. I have only wanted to see you happy, Varya. Happy and safe.'

Varya nodded, her eyes still holding too much sorrow. Too much experience. She spoke again, and Grigori translated.

'She says she wants to see Sergei happy as well.' Varya glanced consideringly at Hannah and spoke again. Grigori blushed as he translated, 'She asks him if he will be happy with you.'

Hannah drew her breath in sharply, wondering what Sergei would say. He turned to give her a long, considering look that made her flush.

'Very,' he said quietly, in English, and no one spoke for a long moment after that.

They left the hospital in a quiet, contemplative mood, and ate lunch in a restaurant near Red Square. Hannah could see the spires of St Basil's from her seat and wondered what would have happened if those kids hadn't pickpocketed her. If Sergei hadn't intervened.

Her life, she mused, would probably have stayed very much the same, struggling on in the shop, determined to make it work and trying not to acknowledge how unhappy it all made her.

She turned to Sergei. 'I need to return to New York.'

He stilled, glancing at her warily. 'When?'

'Soon. In the next week, at least.'

'I see.' Sergei's voice was neutral, perhaps even cool, and Hannah couldn't tell what he was thinking.

'I need to take care of things with the shop,' she explained.

'Do you want me to come with you?' Sergei asked after a moment, and Hannah was moved that he would consider such a thing.

'No. You have work to do here. And I think I need to do this alone.'

He gave her another wary look, swiftly veiled, and then nodded. 'Of course.'

'It should,' Hannah offered hesitantly, 'only take a week or so.'

Sergei nodded. 'And then you'll come back,' he said, and

Hannah had the odd feeling that he was telling himself as much as her.

'Yes,' she said. 'I'll come back.'

It was strange to be back in Hadley Springs. It felt so small, so narrow, and Hannah's whole world had changed in the meantime. She dumped her bag back in the house, which felt musty and unused, still filled with her parents' furniture and possessions, things that had never really been her own. Funny how she'd never considered that until now.

After changing and washing her face she headed over to the shop, its window bright and welcoming with a new display of colourful balls of wools artfully arranged in a selection of wicker baskets.

'Hannah!' Lisa came from behind the counter to give her a big hug, the bells on the door still jangling.

'Hi, Lisa.' Hannah returned the hug, glancing admiringly around the shop. 'You've done some things differently.'

'I hope you don't mind—'

'Mind? Of course not. It looks fantastic.'

Lisa had brought in a pair of comfortable chintz chairs for the corner by the window, with a little table between them and a selection of knitting magazines and patterns laid out for customers to peruse. There was a sign offering coffee along with the evening knitting classes, and the whole place had a more cheerful, happy, lived-in feel. Lisa *liked* being here, Hannah realised, and she never had. What a difference it made.

'So,' Lisa said, propping her elbows on the counter, 'tell me all about it.'

Hannah smiled wryly. All she'd told Lisa before she left was that she had an opportunity to go away for a week and she thought she needed a break. Lisa had agreed with alacrity, and Hannah had been able to tell by the knowing glint in her friend's eyes that she suspected a man was involved.

'It's been a pretty intense time,' Hannah said now. 'Intense and incredible.' Which was an understatement.

'So there *was* a man,' Lisa said with a grin. 'You don't have intense and incredible weeks on your own.'

'Don't you?' Hannah teased, then gave a little laugh. 'All right, yes, there was—is—a man. An amazing man.'

'You want to tell me who it is?'

'I'll tell you all about it,' Hannah promised. 'Over dinner, my treat. And,' she added slowly, looking around the shop once more, 'I have something else to ask you too.'

Several hours—and a bottle of wine—later, it was amazingly all settled. Hannah had told Lisa all about Sergei, and Lisa had agreed—enthusiastically—to buy Hannah's shop.

'I don't care about the money,' Hannah said, and Lisa shook her head.

'You should,' she said firmly. 'I'm not going to stiff you, Hannah, for heaven's sake, even if you end up marrying a billionaire.'

Hannah's heart lurched at that thought. 'It hasn't got nearly that far yet,' she said quietly. 'It's still very new.'

Lisa reached over to squeeze her hand. 'But you love him, don't you?'

'Yes.' There was, Hannah thought, no question about that.

Later that night Hannah went back to the shop. She walked slowly through the office and the stock room, finally stopping in the middle of the shop itself. The wind rattled the windowpane and the moon cast a swathe of silver on the floor.

She was glad Lisa was buying the shop, glad it would have the kind of chance her parents had wanted. She was glad to let go of the anger and resentment she'd nurtured this last year and maybe even longer than that without realising it.

Her parents had loved this shop, but they'd loved her too. She knew that, felt it deep in her bones. And even if they'd made unwise financial decisions—even if her mother had lied to her about staying at college—Hannah knew she could let it go. She could forgive.

She could move on. Just as Sergei had.

Smiling faintly, she flicked out the lights before slipping outside and closing the door.

Sergei stared irritably at the sheaf of papers spread out on his desk, the figures blurring before his tired eyes. He hadn't slept well in a week—since Hannah had gone. Her absence was the reason for his restless irritation now, and the thought both unsettled and humbled him. He still wasn't used to feeling so much, for one woman.

He'd only rung her once since she'd left. She'd seemed as if she wanted to be left alone to deal with what remained of her life in New York; Sergei didn't think there was much. He wished she'd agreed to have him accompany her back to the States; he wished she'd wanted him to come.

Sighing, Sergei rubbed a hand over his eyes and tried to focus on the figures. He'd spent far too much of this last week acting like a lovelorn idiot…and wondering if and when Hannah would return.

His intercom buzzed, and Sergei pressed Talk. 'Yes?'

'There is a woman who wishes to see you—' Grigori began, and Sergei, his heart lurching with uneasy, impossible hope, cut him off.

'Send her in.'

He had half risen from his desk, the smile ready on his face, hoping to see Hannah, when a stranger walked through his door.

Almost a stranger.

Sergei stared at the young woman with her blonde hair tied back in a neat ponytail, her eyes very wide and very blue… as blue as his.

His smile faded as he stared at her, drank her in, his heart beating painfully. *'Alyona?'*

'You're…Sergei Kholodov?'

'Yes.' Of course she didn't recognise him. Sergei came from behind the desk and, as formally as if this were a business meeting, extended his hand for her to shake. 'Are you… Allison Whitelaw?'

'Yes.' She shook his hand and then quickly let go. 'You must think I'm mad, coming here unannounced like this.'

'I am surprised, yes,' Sergei replied. 'But also very glad to see you. Did you…did you come all the way from America?'

She chewed her lip, her nervous gaze sweeping downwards. 'Yes. I know it was terribly impulsive. My parents don't even know I'm here. But—I felt I had to see you, not just email or talk over the phone.' She glanced upwards, uncertain and yet curious. 'I'm sorry to barge in—'

'No, it is fine. Perfectly fine. Come and sit down…if you like.'

'Okay.' She perched on the edge of a leather sofa, and Sergei sat across from her in a chair. Neither of them spoke for several long, tense moments. Sergei felt his throat close up, his eyes sting. He had waited for this moment for twenty-two years, and yet he hadn't expected it to happen like this. He hadn't let himself think about it very much all, but he realised now he'd hoped—secretly—that Alyona would have at least remembered him. It was clear from the wary way she gazed at him that she didn't.

'I told that detective guy—whoever he was—I didn't want contact because I was so freaked out,' she confessed in a rush, sounding so very American. 'I didn't even know I had a brother.'

Sergei swallowed. 'I see.'

'My parents didn't either,' she continued, and Sergei said nothing. She gulped and then said, slowly now, 'But after received that email—well, I couldn't stop thinking about it. About you.' She gazed at him openly now, reminding him so much—so painfully—of the little girl she'd once been.

I'm not scared, Serozhya. Not when I'm with you.

I'm not coming this time, Alyona. But you'll be all right, I know you will.

'I started having these...memories,' Alyona—Allison—continued. 'Memories I didn't even know I had. Little things. A—a stuffed animal—a cat.' She stared at him, a question in her eyes, and Sergei forced himself to speak past the lump in his throat.

'You had a little toy like that,' he confirmed softly. 'You called him Leo.'

'Leo,' Allison repeated. 'Short for...' She paused, the words seeming almost to form themselves. 'Short for Leontiy.'

Sergei's heart seemed to do a somersault. 'Yes, after our father. And since it was a cat, Leo seemed like a good name.'

'Right.' They both lapsed into silence, the memories heavy between them. 'And other things,' Allison finally said. 'Flowers.'

'Snowdrops,' Sergei told her. 'I used to pick them for you. They grew in the corner of the yard, just a few raggedy ones.'

She smiled, shyly, and then suddenly blurted, 'Why...why were we separated?'

Sergei hesitated, knowing he had to answer carefully. He did not want to sow discord between his sister and her adoptive parents; no good would come of that. 'I was fourteen when you were adopted,' he finally said. 'Generally only younger children are chosen for adoption. It is too difficult for older children to adjust to a new family, a new culture.'

She frowned. 'But if my parents had known I had a brother, they would have adopted you as well. I know they would have.'

Sergei said nothing, and Allison's eyes narrowed in a way

that was achingly familiar. Even as a child she'd been hard to fool. 'You think they knew,' she said quietly. 'And didn't choose you.'

'I did not want to find you in order to discuss this,' Sergei said. 'I wanted—'

'They didn't.' Allison leaned forward, her eyes blazing with determination. 'They didn't know, Serozyha. I promise you, they were *shocked*—'

Sergei stared at her. 'What did you just call me?'

'Sss—Serozhya.' She blinked, surprised, and Sergei felt himself smiling. She remembered. She might not even realise she did, but he knew the truth. She remembered him. 'I wish you would believe my parents didn't know,' she said after a moment. 'I think it would make a difference.'

'It makes no difference now. It was over twenty years ago.'

'Doesn't it?' She gazed at him with a compassionate perceptiveness that reminded him of Hannah. 'All these years, to think we were separated on purpose because they only wanted me, and not you?' She reached over and laid her hand, slender and soft, on his. 'It wasn't like that. They didn't know. Perhaps it was the language barrier, or a mix-up at the orphanage…'

Or a system that was overburdened, disorganised, and corrupt. Or even a director who had never liked the surly boy who wouldn't be cowed or bullied, the boy he knew he'd be able to kick out onto the street in just eighteen months. There could be a dozen reasons, and yet—

Sergei swallowed, didn't speak.

'I told them about the email,' Allison continued, 'and they were concerned. They wanted to make sure you were genuine.'

'Naturally.'

'They thought it might be some kind of scam,' she explained. 'But when I started having these memories, and then they saw you were quite well known and, well, you know, rich—' She gave a little laugh, embarrassed. 'All I mean is they knew you weren't after their money.'

'Right.'

She gave him a sad smile. 'But I wish you'd believe they didn't know about you back then. They were so shocked, and angry too, because they had no idea. I looked it up online, it's happened more than once—siblings who were separated without the adoptive parents knowing—'

Words tumbled into Sergei's mind. *And I find it better to believe in people and live in hope than become as jaded and cynical as you obviously are.*

But he wasn't jaded any more. Hannah had seen to that. And even if he'd been willing to believe the worst of his sister's family for over twenty years, he realised he didn't want to any more. Now he chose hope. Willingly, deliberately. He smiled at Allison. 'Maybe,' he said slowly, 'I do believe.'

She smiled, her whole face lightening. 'They want to meet you.'

That surprised—and moved—him. Made him a little sad too, for all they might have missed. 'Do they?'

'Yes, of course. Just think. All these years—we could have been a family.'

A family. Something he'd never had. He'd had a grandmother who hated him, parents who had never bothered to be around, a sister who had been taken from him far too young.

A family. Yet now was not the time for regrets, Sergei knew. He had a family now, a family of two. He had Hannah. And who knew, perhaps he had Alyona too, and her parents. A different kind of family, but a family all the same.

'I'd like to meet them,' he told Allison, and meant it. 'But first, since you came all this way, I'd like to hear all about you.' And he settled back in his chair to listen.

* * *

It felt good to be back in Moscow. Right. Hannah breathed in the warm spring air as she hailed a cab—a metered one—outside the airport.

She threw her suitcase in the trunk and slid inside, giving Sergei's work address. It was ten o'clock in the morning, and she knew he'd be at work. At least she hoped he'd be at work. She was dying to see him. She'd missed him this last week, especially since they'd barely spoken. He'd rung once, to make sure she'd arrived safely, and Hannah had left a message on his mobile to say she was on her way back. Her way home.

She leaned back against the seat as the taxi sped towards the city centre. She was glad, in a way, that they'd had this week apart, this week of virtually no contact, because she felt they'd both needed it to process and test their feelings. Everything had happened so quickly and intensely, it was hard to trust it was real. Believe it could last.

But now she did…and she hoped Sergei did too.

Grigori half rose from his desk when Hannah entered the reception area in front of Sergei's office. 'Hannah—'

She smiled, genuinely glad to see him. 'How are you? And Varya?'

'She is recovering. She allows me to take care of her, and that is enough for me.' He smiled. 'Still the mouse in the box, but it is a comfortable place. I don't mind.'

'I'm glad,' Hannah said. She did not offer platitudes that Varya might come to love him in time; there were no guarantees. But she hoped and prayed so, for Grigori's sake. For Varya's too. She nodded towards the closed doors of Sergei's office. 'Is he in?'

'Yes—'

She smiled mischievously. 'Do you think I should surprise him?'

Grigori smiled back, just as mischievous. 'Yes.'

Hannah knocked once on the door before turning the handle and slipping inside.

'Who—?' Sergei glanced up from his papers, frowning, and stopped when he saw Hannah. She gazed back at him, amazed and a little afraid by how absolutely good it was to see him. How much she'd missed him. It had only been one week, after all.

Sergei rose from the desk. 'You're back,' he said, without much expression at all, and Hannah cocked her head in acknowledgement.

'I said about a week.'

'I know, but—' He moved from behind the desk, crossed the room in three great strides and then pulled Hannah into his arms. After he'd kissed her thoroughly enough to obliterate any remaining uncertainty or doubt, he pulled back, gazing down at her soberly. 'I missed you. I didn't like it.'

She laid her hand against his cheek. 'You didn't? Why not?'

'I don't like missing people,' Sergei said, his voice a little hoarse. 'I've tried not to miss anyone or let them matter for years, and I just can't do that with you.'

Emotion welled inside her and she smiled rather tremulously. 'I'm glad.'

'So am I,' he said, and kissed her again.

He took her out to dinner that night, to celebrate Alyona's return and the sale of her shop. They'd caught up on all that had happened over coffee in Sergei's office, and then later in bed at his penthouse as the sun sent its late golden beams across the tangled sheets.

Now as the limo pulled to the front of The Kholodov, Hannah glanced at Sergei. 'Where—?'

'You'll see.'

He led her through the opulent lobby, reminding her of how impressed—and intimidated—she'd been a year ago. How she hadn't been able to stop thinking of him. Wanting him.

She still couldn't.

The little private booth was the same, with its candlelight and crystal, and as Sergei led her to the table Hannah had a strange sense of déjà vu. Yet at the same time everything was different. So wonderfully different.

They lingered over their meal, savouring the food and wine and simply being together, and, while the same bubbles of expectation buoyed her as they had before, nervous anticipation had been replaced by a deeper joy.

After the dishes were cleared away Sergei rose from the table, and Hannah glanced at him in surprise. 'What—'

'I'm going to do it right this time.'

'Right?' she repeated blankly, then stopped in surprise for Sergei had sunk to one knee.

'Hannah Pearl, I love you completely. You've changed me for ever, made me see and feel things I'd never thought to again. You've allowed me to believe, to hope once more, and that alone is precious.' He took a breath, his eyes blazing with the light of his love as Hannah felt tears sting her own. 'But you've given me more than that. You've given me love, and laughter, and you haven't let me intimidate you even when I try, because the honest truth is you scare me so much.'

Hannah let out a little laugh, tears trembling on her lids. Sergei gazed up at her seriously.

'I'm new to this, to loving someone like this, and it scares me. I won't get it right, I'll drive you half-mad, and I can only ask you to bear with me. Believe the best in me, which you told me you did, much to my own amazement.'

'I do,' Hannah said softly. 'Oh, Sergei, I do.'

'Then,' Sergei said, taking out a small box of black velvet, 'will you do me the great honour of becoming my wife?'

Hannah swallowed, joy and disbelief and just pure emotion welling up like a fountain inside her. Until she'd seen Sergei again she hadn't realised how nervous she'd been that he might have changed his mind. His heart. And until he'd said all those wonderful things, she hadn't been completely sure he'd felt them.

Now she was sure. She was very, very sure. 'Yes,' she whispered, and then her voice grew stronger. 'Yes, I'll marry you.'

Sergei took the ring, a gorgeous diamond flanked by sapphires, and slipped it on her finger. He rose to his feet and kissed her, his arms coming around her, pulling her close. They remained there for a few moments, in the circle of each other's arms, Hannah's cheek resting against his shoulder, the room quiet and still and filled with a gentle peace.

Then, with a little smile, Sergei tugged her towards the door, and upstairs, to the sumptuous suite she'd stayed in once before, where the rest of their lives would now begin.

* * * * *

A sneaky peek at next month...

MODERN™

INTERNATIONAL AFFAIRS, SEDUCTION & PASSION GUARANTEED

My wish list for next month's titles...

In stores from 18th November 2011:

☐ Jewel in His Crown – Lynne Graham

☐ Once a Ferrara Wife... – Sarah Morgan

☐ In Bed with a Stranger – India Grey

☐ The Call of the Desert – Abby Green

☐ How to Win the Dating War – Aimee Carson

In stores from 2nd December 2011:

☐ The Man Every Woman Wants – Miranda Lee

☐ Not Fit for a King? – Jane Porter

☐ In a Storm of Scandal – Kim Lawrence

☐ Playing His Dangerous Game – Tina Duncan

☐ Acquired: The CEO's Small-Town Bride – Catherine Mann

Available at WHSmith, Tesco, Asda, Eason, Amazon and Apple

1111/01

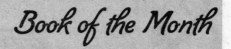

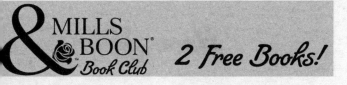

MILLS & BOON® Book Club

2 Free Books!

Get your free books now at

www.millsandboon.co.uk/freebookoffer

Or fill in the form below and post it back to us

THE MILLS & BOON® BOOK CLUB™—HERE'S HOW IT WORKS: Accepting your free books places you under no obligation to buy anything. You may keep the books and return the despatch note marked 'Cancel'. If we do not hear from you, about a month later we'll send you 4 brand-new stories from the Modern™ series priced at £3.30* each. There is no extra charge for post and packaging. You may cancel at any time, otherwise we will send you 4 stories a month which you may purchase or return to us—the choice is yours. *Terms and prices subject to change without notice. Offer valid in UK only. Applicants must be 18 or over. Offer expires 28th February 2012. **For full terms and conditions, please go to www.millsandboon.co.uk/termsandconditions**

Mrs/Miss/Ms/Mr (please circle) _____

First Name _____

Surname _____

Address _____

_____

_____ Postcode _____

E-mail _____

Send this completed page to: Mills & Boon Book Club, Free Book Offer, FREEPOST NAT 10298, Richmond, Surrey, TW9 1BR

Find out more at
www.millsandboon.co.uk/freebookoffer

Visit us Online

0611/P1ZEE

ag